Days That End in Y

by VIKKI VanSICKLE

Scholastic Canada Ltd.

Toronto New York London Auckland Sydney
Mexico City New Delhi Hong Kong Buenos Aires

Scholastic Canada Ltd.
604 King Street West, Toronto, Ontario M5V 1E1, Canada

Scholastic Inc.
557 Broadway, New York, NY 10012, USA

Scholastic Australia Pty Limited
PO Box 579, Gosford, NSW 2250, Australia

Scholastic New Zealand Limited
Private Bag 94407, Botany, Manukau 2163, New Zealand

Scholastic Children's Books
Euston House, 24 Eversholt Street, London NW1 1DB, UK

www.scholastic.ca

Library and Archives Canada Cataloguing in Publication
VanSickle, Vikki, 1982-
Days that end in Y / by Vikki VanSickle.
Issued also in electronic format.
ISBN 978-1-4431-2432-4
I. Title.
PS8643.A59D39 2013   jC813'.6   C2012-905509-3

Cover image © bodhihill.

6 5 4 3 2 1   Printed in Canada 121   13 14 15 16 17

To Rob Kempson:
I wish I had known you when I was twelve.

Canada Day

For some people, summer starts with a bang. Literally. The annual Canada Day fireworks display kicks off two months of lemonade, flip-flops and, most important, freedom.

Canada Day has always been a quiet affair around my place; just me, Mom, Benji and Denise, sitting on the roof, eating popcorn and watching the fireworks. Most people in town head down to Victoria Park to watch them, but who wants to be in the middle of all the noise and the mess when you can lie back on your own roof where it's quiet and peaceful? Well, except for Denise. She can't keep quiet for more than two minutes at a time. But I'll take motormouth Denise over a park full of screaming kids any day. But this year Mom has a boyfriend, and Doug has other ideas about how to spend a perfect Canada Day.

"You mean you've never been to the fireworks?" Doug asks.

"Nope."

"Ever?"

"Never."

"Whoa." Doug runs his hands through his hair, like I just blew his mind. "You don't know what you've been missing!"

"I know exactly what I've been missing: big, noisy crowds. Here, it's just us on the roof: our own private viewing."

"It's like a big party down there! Come on, C-Dog. It'll be fun, I promise! Please?"

Doug looks at me with sad puppy eyes that would put his dog Suzy to shame. Mom is pretty taken with him, and since he seems to be around for the long haul, I am trying to be patient.

"Fine. But don't expect me to enjoy myself."

"I think you'll be surprised," Doug says.

Doubtful.

"I think it's a great change of pace," Mom says, giving Doug's arm a squeeze. "I know Denise will be game, and I'm sure your friends will be, too. Live a little, Clarissa!"

I don't know anybody else who would consider going to a park to watch fireworks a fine example of "living," but it's clear the decision has been made. As usual, my vote doesn't count.

Doug is so thrilled he actually rubs his palms together in excitement. "Rally your troops. We'll head down around eight to get a good spot."

* * *

"All right, team, let's set up shop somewhere away from the ice cream trucks," Doug says.

"And the playground," I add.

Then Denise pipes up, "And the waterfront. Too many kids jumping in and out of the river. I'm not looking to get soaked, thank you very much."

Denise and I don't often agree, but neither of us likes to be bothered by young children. Doug leads us to the middle of the park, on a gentle slope. He sets up camp chairs for my mom, Denise and himself. My mom lays a blanket out in front of them. Benji, Mattie and I wander over to a picnic table nearby. The sky is still pinky-blue, and it's at least an hour before sundown. We have plenty of time before the fireworks start.

"Want to walk around and see who's here?" Mattie asks.

I'm just getting comfortable and already she wants to move. "Everyone I want to see is right here," I say.

"Except Michael," Benji says, grinning (almost) wickedly. I don't dignify that with an answer.

"There're lots of people here. We probably know some of them. Come on!" Mattie says.

"You go ahead. We'll make sure no one takes the table."

"I'm not going by myself," Mattie pouts. "I guess I'll stay here."

"Sorry we're not as exciting as your boyfriend."

Even in the semi-dark I can see Mattie's neck flush. "Andrew couldn't come."

"Trouble in paradise?" I ask.

Mattie throws herself onto the bench next to me and launches into her latest drama. "Maybe, I don't know! He was supposed to call me, and then he didn't. And when I asked him about tonight he said he was busy but wouldn't tell me with what! It's Canada Day! What could he possibly be doing?"

"Did his family go away for the weekend?" Benji asks, trying to be helpful.

"I don't think so. Their car was in the driveway."

"Were you stalking him?" I know Mattie is boy-crazy, but most people would call staking out a boyfriend's house just plain creepy.

"I wasn't stalking him. I was in the car when my mother drove by, and I just happened to notice that the car was there."

"Sure."

3

"It's true! I only have a week before camp, and then I won't see him all summer! Unless he doesn't care . . ." Mattie trails off, looking miserable.

"Speaking of camp, I can't believe you're leaving me. Aren't you getting a little old for all that camp stuff?"

Mattie frowns. "What do you mean? I have two years left of regular camp, including this one, and then I can apply to be junior staff. You're *never* too old for camp."

"I don't see what's so great about it," I mutter. "It's like school except you have to sleep over. *Outside.*"

Mattie gasps. "Camp is not like school," she says. "There aren't any assignments or essays or teachers."

"But don't you have counsellors that teach you stuff?"

"Well, yes, but you can't just pick up a paddle and start canoeing; someone has to show you how!"

"Someone like a teacher," I point out. "And don't you get badges for things?"

Mattie pauses. "Yes, but it's not like you're graded or anything."

"And aren't there a lot of rules about what you can and can't do?"

"Yes, but everything has rules, not just school. Without rules we'd live in total chaos."

"Is that something Andrew taught you?"

Mattie blushes. Her boyfriend is not only a mathlete, but a physics genius.

"Chaos theory happens to be very interesting and applicable in real world situations," she says.

I cover my ears, blocking out anything that sounds like a definition. "Please, we are not in school. Stop talking like a textbook!"

"I think you would like it if you gave it a chance."

"Camp or physics?"

"*Camp.*"

I don't know. Limited electricity, no TV, no hot showers . . .

If you ask me, people who choose to spend a week or a whole summer away at camp probably wish they still lived in pioneer days. I have no romantic notions about the past. I'll take my air conditioning and HDTV, thank you.

"And Benji, you're no better: signing up to spend your whole summer with those drama kids."

"The Gaslighters," Benji corrects me, using the nickname created for and only used by the youth members of the Gaslight Community Players. "Plus, it's not all day, we're usually done around four. You don't get up til noon, anyways, so that's only a few hours you'll have to fend for yourself."

"There's always Michael," Mattie says slyly. I don't respond. This is her getting back at me for the Andrew comments.

Michael Greenblat and I might be dating. I'm not sure. All I know is he calls me sometimes to go for a walk or to get slushies, and I go to his baseball games. We don't ever touch or talk about whether or not we are dating, so you can see why I'm confused. Mattie is convinced that he is in love with me, but I humiliated him in front of a whole restaurant of people a few months ago, so I can understand why he isn't in any rush to call me his girlfriend.

"Look! There he is."

All three of us sit up and stare in the direction that Mattie is pointing. The crowds are getting thicker, and it's just dark enough now that faces are getting hard to make out. But after some scanning I see that, sure enough, Michael is sitting in a camp chair surrounded by his entire family.

"Go say hi!" Mattie says.

"No."

"Why not?"

"You're all watching me."

"Would it help if we looked the other way?" Benji asks.

Too late. Michael has spotted us. I do a double take, as if I just happened to look up and see him and haven't been staring at him for the past five minutes.

"Go say hi," Mattie hisses. She has never sounded so bossy.

"Fine." I haul myself up off the bench, brush the dust off my shorts and make my way over to where Michael's family is seated, trying to ignore the feeling of Mattie and Benji boring holes into my back with their eyes. When it becomes clear I'm coming to see him, Michael gets up and walks to meet me halfway.

"Hi, Michael."

"Hey, Clarissa."

We smile at each other, neither of us sure what to say.

"So, have you been to the fireworks before?" I ask.

Michael nods. "Every year. You?"

"This is my first time. We usually watch from our roof, but there's so many of us now it would probably collapse if we all tried to sit up there."

I'm not convinced this qualifies as a joke, but Michael laughs anyway. I can't tell if it's out of pity or pure awkwardness.

"Is that Benji?"

I look over my shoulder at my friends, who wave innocently. I glare at them.

"Yeah. And Mattie. Do you want to sit with us?"

Michael looks stricken. "No, no," he answers quickly.

"It's fine. I should probably stay with my family, anyway," he gestures toward them. His mother, who up to this point has been watching our whole conversation with squinted eyes, as if focusing her laser vision on us, suddenly brightens up and waves. I am equally relieved and disappointed that he said no.

"Okay. Well, see you around."

"Sure. If you're not doing anything next Tuesday, maybe you could come to my game?"

"Okay. Sure. I mean, I think I'm not doing anything."

"We play at Ferndale. Seven o'clock."

"Okay, I'll be there."

Michael smiles. He looks relaxed for the first time in this whole conversation.

I make my way back, feeling confused. He wouldn't have invited me to yet another baseball game if he didn't like me, but why wouldn't he sit with me? It's like for every plus there is a negative, leaving me stuck in neutral.

Now *I* sound like the physics genius.

"Well?" Mattie says.

"I asked him to sit with us, but he said no. I think he's a little afraid of me," I confess.

"Do you blame him?" Benji asks. I try to elbow him in the side, but he scooches down the bench, out of the way.

"Just keep doing what you're doing," Mattie says with complete confidence. "Boys have short memories. Soon he'll forget all about The Dairy Bar Incident, and you'll be together by the end of the summer."

"He did invite me to another baseball game."

"What? Why didn't you say that before?" Mattie clutches my arm with both hands. The sudden movement catches the eyes of both Denise and my mom, who have probably also just watched my conversation with Michael. Great. The last thing I need is a summit on the state of Michael and me. Not that there is any Michael and me.

"Ouch! Jeez, let go. I've been twice before. It's no big deal; it's just a baseball game."

"It is not just a baseball game; it's a gesture. It means he's ready to move on from The Dairy Bar Incident." Mattie calms down for one second to pout. "No fair — I'm about to go to camp just as you're about to embark on a romantic summer."

"Don't get your hopes up. I can't think of anything less romantic than a baseball game."

Benji starts humming the song "Summer Nights" from the movie *Grease* and bopping his shoulders like he is a girl in a poodle skirt from the 1950s. I roll my eyes, but obviously it isn't a big enough gesture because Mattie joins right in, and soon the two of them are dancing around the picnic table, doo-wopping their way through the number.

"I get it," I say. "Summer loving. Ha, ha."

Mattie stops, her hand over her heart. "What you have is so much more than just summer loving," she says. "You and Michael are forever."

If only I had something to throw at her. But I don't. So I end up bopping along with them. "Summer Nights" is a very catchy song.

BOOM!

The crowd gasps as the first firework of the night explodes across the sky in a burst of yellow and red.

"Come on!" We hurry back to where the rest of our little party is seated, spreading ourselves across the blanket my mother laid out. I have to admit, watching the fireworks at the park is pretty great. It's kind of corny, but I like how everyone *oohs* and *aahs* together as the coloured lights explode above us. I thought it might get annoying, but it turns out it's a nice feeling. It adds a real sense of occasion to the fireworks. I love the moment between the boom of the firework taking off and the burst of colour and light. Each time I find myself holding my breath, just a little, until the streaks and swirls and stipples of light appear like magic in the sky. Doug calls out the names of the fireworks.

"You see that? That's called a Roman candle."

"That there is a spider; see how it looks like legs?"

"And that magnificent display is probably a crossette."

It's still hot out, but the grass is cool and that makes the temperature bearable. The display goes on for about half an hour. It's a nice feeling, being surrounded by friends but not having to say anything. My mind wanders a bit, and I feel like I'm in two places: watching the fireworks, but also deep in my head, wondering about Michael. When the finale kicks in, the noise is deafening, and the display is so bright it casts red and yellows shadows across my friends' faces. It seems like the organizers took every single firework and shot them up at the same time, pinwheels and sunbursts and spiders spiralling across the sky and then fading into nothing.

After the whizzing and popping has stopped, puffs of coloured smoke twist in the sky. Nobody moves, hoping for one last encore. When it becomes clear that the show is done for another year, conversations pick up again and people start moving toward the parking lot, clogging the sidewalks and paths like ants on a mission. I stay where I am, stretching my arms and legs until the knots in my spine pop and sigh.

"I love fireworks," Benji says. "Don't you?"

"Yeah."

"Isn't this a perfect night?" Mattie adds. "Couldn't you stay here forever? You know, Clarissa, we do this kind of thing at camp all the time. Except instead of fireworks we go stargazing. I really think you should reconsider—"

"Mattie, stop!" I groan, rolling away from her camp pep talk. "You're ruining the moment."

I get to my knees, look back at my mother, and then I freeze. Doug is kneeling in the grass in front of my mother's chair, holding a little, dark box in his hands. I don't need x-ray vision to know there's a ring inside.

Engagement Day

As soon as she realizes what's going on, Mattie grasps the arm of my t-shirt and starts murmuring, "Oh my gosh, oh my gosh, oh my gosh," under her breath. I wrench my arm free.

"*Shhh,*" I hiss.

It's hard to hear what Doug's saying, but you don't have to be a genius to get the gist of it. He's got a ring; he's asking her to marry him. I creep closer, Mattie glued to one side and Benji clutching my hand. Part of me wants to shake them off, but the whole situation is so unbelievable that I also kind of need their physical presence to ground me.

". . . and maybe this seems rash or sudden, but I've known for a long time that you were the one, and I was just wondering—"

Mom cuts him off, leaping out of her chair onto the ground, throwing her arms around him. "Yes! Yes, you wonderful man!"

Denise is frozen, one hand covering her mouth, the other holding a camp chair tucked under her arm. She is obviously just as shocked as I am. Mattie is the first person to react, somehow managing to jump up and down, squeal and hug me at the same time. When my mom and Doug manage to untangle themselves, she launches herself at my mom, crying, "Congratulations, Annie! This is so exciting!"

I watch the moment unfold, feeling strangely separate from it. A good daughter would jump up and down and cry and hug her mother and congratulate her, like Mattie. But I feel like I just met Doug. And I've never had a man living in my house before. Then, all I can think about is what if I run into Doug on his way out of the shower in a towel? Or, worse, what if I'm the one in a towel? It's bound to happen eventually. And where will all his giant-sized stuff (shoes, tubs of protein powder, family-size boxes of cereal) go?

Beside me, Benji whispers, "Are you okay?"

"I'm fine, just surprised."

Now other people have started to clue in, and complete strangers come up to pat Doug on the back or offer to take pictures. Denise has tears streaming down her face, and at one point someone mistakes her for the teary, but joyful, lucky bride-to-be. That's almost funny enough to knock me out of my stupor, but I still feel like I've been struck dumb, like maybe the fireworks messed with the wiring of my brain.

Mom takes a breather from all her smiling and posing and catches my eye. Seeing how happy she is melts my frozen legs, and I run over to join in the celebrations. She gives me a full strength hug, and then Doug joins in, and before I know it, I'm caught in the middle of a hugging sandwich. Doug lifts both me and Mom off the ground in his giant arms, causing Mom to squeal and my head to pound. It's nice, if a little weird, and I wonder if group hugs are going to become a regular thing in my life now.

When Doug puts us down he throws both arms in the air, fists clenched in victory, and crows like a rooster, "I got the girl!"

It's more than a little embarrassing.

As a group, we are some of the last people out of the park. We walk Mattie and Denise home first — which is a relief, since the two of them discussing appropriate train length and wedding invitation etiquette is exhausting — then Benji and I drop back behind my mom and Doug, leaving them to stroll hand-in-hand and discuss the future on their own.

"Hey! You're going to have a dog now!" Benji says.

Cripes. I forgot about Suzy. As if living with Doug isn't going to be strange enough.

"You say that like it's a good thing," I grumble.

"Most people like dogs," Benji points out.

"I think I might be a cat person."

"You could grow to love her."

"Doubtful."

"Either way, she's going to live with you now."

The way he says it makes it sound like a proclamation of absolute finality. It sends a shiver across my shoulders. Doug is moving in. So is Suzy. My house will become his house. I guess, technically, it'll be *our* house. But it's been *my* house for so long, that I have trouble inserting Doug and his dog into the picture. There will be pet food in the cupboards, a water dish that will slop all over the floor and dog hair on absolutely everything.

Nobody better expect me to poop-and-scoop.

***

I'm not even close to being asleep when Mom knocks at my door later that night.

"Come in," I say.

She enters tentatively, peering around the door and whispering, "Did I wake you?"

"No. I'm not very sleepy."

"No, I imagine there's a lot on your mind." Mom smiles and sits on the edge of my bed, careful not to touch me. Instead, she straightens my sheets, smoothing them over and over like she has a tic. Her eyes occasionally reach me. She's sizing me up, trying to figure out how freaked out I am. Finally, when the sheets can't possibly be any smoother, she says, "I wanted to talk to you about tonight. We haven't had a moment to ourselves all evening."

"Okay."

"That was a shocker, huh?"

"You mean you didn't know he was going to ask you?"

"We'd talked about it. Getting married, I mean," Mom admits. Then she adds, "But, no, I didn't know he was planning on asking me tonight." Her gaze wanders down to her fingers, where her brand new ring sits, demanding attention. She wiggles her fingers, and the diamond catches the light and throws it in big sparkles across the bedroom wall. I watch them, thinking about how they look like fireworks: bright and temporary. Just hours ago I was at the fireworks with my mom and her boyfriend. Now he's her fiancé.

"Hello? Are you in there?" Mom knocks gently on my head with her fingers, and I release a big gush of air I didn't realize I was holding.

"I'm here," I say, stalling.

"What are you thinking?" Mom looks both nervous and hopeful, which prompts me to speak.

"It's going to be weird with a boy in the house," I say, being as honest as I can without sounding selfish or too unsure about the whole thing.

Mom nods. "I know. It's been just us girls for so long. It'll be weird at first, but good, too. Right?"

"Right," I agree, adding, "I do like Doug."

Mom smiles. "I know you do, but it's okay to feel strange about it. This is big."

"Super big."

"The biggest."

Well, not the biggest. The biggest thing that has happened to us in the past few years was her breast cancer diagnosis. She's been healthy and cancer-free for over a year now, but it doesn't seem like so long ago that I woke up every day and thought about my mother dying. I can tell by her silence that mom is thinking about it, too. Enough doom and gloom. This is her engagement day!

"When is the wedding?" I ask, trying to brighten things up a little.

"At the end of the summer."

I'm glad I was sitting for that part. "But that's less than two months away. Don't people take, like, a whole year to plan a wedding?"

"Neither of us wants a big to-do: just a little backyard party with our closest friends. You're welcome to invite some of your friends: Benji, Mattie, even Michael, if you want."

"Are you going to get a dress?"

"Probably, but nothing fancy."

"Denise is going to be upset. She likes a big wedding."

"Denise will be thrilled that I'm not stuffing her into a hideous bridesmaid's dress."

Too bad. *That* I would like to see.

"When is he moving in?"

"We thought he'd move in in stages. He's going to start bringing some boxes by next weekend. That gives you and me some time to do a little cleaning and make room."

"That's soon," I say carefully, not wanting to let on that I am anything but thrilled about it.

"Why wait?" Mom says with a goofy smile I have come to think of as her Doug smile. "It's something we both want."

In my head I'm thinking, but what about what I want? What's wrong with how things are now? Can't two people live separately and still be in love? Wouldn't that be the perfect situation? You wouldn't have to clean up after the other person or get annoyed by their habits. Living separately seems like it would be the best way to *stay* in love.

Of course, I don't say any of this out loud. Judging by the look on my mother's face, I can tell she wouldn't agree. It's like her Doug smile has melted her entire face, turning it into a sappy, goofy mess.

Mom tucks my hair behind my ears and leans in for a quick hug. The hug is short but tight, and I can tell how happy she is by how hard she squeezes me.

"This is a big step, baby," she says, her words tickling my ears. "It's a whole new world for the Delaney girls."

When she pulls back, she smiles at me — a true Annie smile, not a Doug smile — and I return it. When Annette Delaney smiles at you, it's near impossible to not smile back. It's like a magnet that tugs at the corners of your mouth until, before you know it, you're grinning right back. Even if your insides are all mixed up.

Cleaning Day

With Doug all set to officially move in, Mom is on a cleaning spree to make room for all his man-stuff. Whenever she gets a spare moment, she attacks a corner of the house, throwing everything into a "keep" pile or a "Salvation Army" pile. I'm supposed to be helping, but she's such a furious organizer that most of the time I just end up keeping her company.

Today her last client rescheduled, so she's using the free time to attack her closet. It's less interesting than the shed — which we gutted last night. We found toys I hadn't used in ages, a bird's nest and half a mouse. That was a little gross, but fascinating. Where did the other half go? What kind of cruel animal leaves half a mouse behind?

I'm sitting on the bed, trying to avoid being hit in the face by the blouses and belts that fly by as Mom de-clutters her closet.

"Can you believe I ever wore this colour? This must have been a gift. Or an impulse buy."

"It looks like something Denise would buy," I joke.

Mom gasps and pulls out a red dress I've never seen before. In fact, it doesn't look like anything else she owns. It has buttons down the front and is belted across the waist, like a long, tailored shirt. "I forgot about this dress! I wonder if it still fits?" She holds it against her body and looks in the full-length mirror that hangs on the back of her closet door.

"What's it from?"

"This was my interview dress. Everyone else would show up in grey skirts and suits, and I'd waltz in wearing red." Mom smiles and I can imagine her breezing into a room of boring, serious people looking like a movie star.

"Interview for what?"

"Jobs, baby. They don't just hand them out for free."

I never really thought of my mom working anywhere but at the Hair Emporium. As far as I knew, she left high school, had me, spent a few years at a mall salon perfecting her skills and then opened up her own place.

"When was this?"

Mom shrugs. "I worked all through high school and then just before you were born."

"What kind of jobs?"

"This and that. Receptionist, sales associate, nothing fancy. You need a degree to get a fancy job," she waggles her finger at me, "which is why you are going to university."

Not this conversation again. "Can I go to high school first?"

Mom laughs. "Deal." She hugs the dress to her body one more time and says, "I just can't part with this yet. Doug will have to suffer with a little less space in the closet."

I still haven't quite recovered from the image of my mother answering phones somewhere downtown. "But you like being a stylist, right?"

"Of course! I love the Hair Emporium almost as much as I love you." Mom smiles wryly and adds, "Sometimes even more."

"More than Doug?" I ask.

"Be nice." The phone rings before I can get a lecture. On

her way to answer it, Mom dumps a box on the bed beside me. "Here. Make yourself useful."

Most of the box is old magazines and a few books — romance novels with a few murder mysteries thrown in for variety. I am about to haul the whole thing to the Salvation Army pile, when I spot what looks like a yearbook. I dig around in the box, and sure enough, there are four yearbooks. All are bright red leather with "Sir John A. Macdonald Secondary School" stamped in yellow on the front. Mom's old yearbooks! I feel like I've found a winning lottery ticket.

"That was Doug," Mom says, returning from her phone call. "He's bringing Chinese for dinner—" Mom stops short when she sees the yearbook in my hands. "Oh my god, where did you find those?"

"In the box you gave me."

Mom sits on the bed next to me, tucking her feet under her like a teenager.

"I haven't seen these in ages! May I?"

I give her the yearbook, and she flips through the pages, shaking her head and murmuring under her breath. It's almost like I'm not there; it's just her and the yearbook strolling down memory lane. "This is wild. Look how young we were!"

"Wow," I say, as she points out people I've never met before. I am itching to look at the books myself, but I act bored. I know my mother, and it is not wise to show too much interest or she'll get suspicious.

"Are you going to throw these out?" I ask.

Mom looks horrified. "Of course not! Put them in the keep pile, and I'll make room for them somewhere. I'm sure Doug will get a kick out of them. Denise, too." Mom frowns. "On second thought, I think Denise got rid of her yearbooks a few years ago when she was reinventing herself. Something about ghosts of the past holding her back." Mom and I share a smile, which is nice. Smiles at the expense of Denise are rare. Mom is Denise's number one defender and rarely acknowledges her crazy factor, which is significant.

Mom smiles wistfully at me and tucks a strand of hair behind my ear, even though it doesn't need to be smoothed. "Just think, in a few weeks you'll be embarking on your own high school years."

"Don't remind me," I mutter. I'm not the biggest fan of school, and a new school that's three times as big as my old one, where I'll be the lowest form of life, is even less appealing. Mom is quiet, and when I turn to see what's up, there are tears in her eyes.

"Mom, what's wrong?"

"You're just so big. You used to be my baby, and now look at you!"

Mom-tears make me uncomfortable. I look away, pretending to be busy folding and refolding a blazer until the coast is clear. When Mom starts humming, I look up again. I don't recognize the song; probably something from the "good old days." I eye the yearbooks but continue to fold the clothes she tosses my way.

When the door opens and Doug yells, "Who's hungry? I've got chow mein!" I let her run ahead. Then I fish the books out of the keep pile and smuggle them to my room where I can examine them later.

I tell myself that everything is fine; it's not stealing if it's from your own house and you intend to return something eventually. Right?

Dog Day

After stuffing ourselves full of Chinese food, Mom and Doug go outside to have a beer on the porch. I sneak off to my bedroom to find out about my mother's past.

I have one big reason for wanting to be alone with the yearbooks: my dad. I've never even seen a picture of him. Over the years I've learned bits and pieces from Denise — like how all the girls loved his floppy hair, how charming he was and that he met my mother at a bush party. But I could still count all the things I knew about him on one hand. It's never bothered me before — not much, anyway — but now that I have the chance to look him up, I can barely contain myself.

I skip the yearbooks from grades nine and ten and go straight to the year my parents met, grade eleven. I know Bill switched schools for her, moving from Bennington to Sir John A. so they could spend more time together. Imagine someone being so in love with you that he went to the trouble of switching schools!

Someone else's yearbook is not as exciting as you might imagine: page after page of school photos arranged in rows, some "wacky" club photos, a few news articles from the local paper and a list of notable world events that happened that year. You don't realize how old your parents are until you discover that things you learned about in history class happened when they were in high school.

Everyone has one of three haircuts, and none of them are flattering: flat-ironed paper thin locks, shags gone wrong and big bangs. I scan the page of students with last names that start with D–F, and there she is, the Dairy Queen. Even with an overly layered haircut it's hard to find fault with Annette Delaney. With her heart-shaped face, dimples and eyes that sparkle, even in black and white, she has a face that looks made to smile. All the other girls on the page look like regular teenagers, but Annie Delaney looks like a teenager from a movie.

Obviously someone else felt the same way, because there is an arrow pointing to the picture with the words *Eat your heart out, Jeff K!* scrawled in the margin. The same person (I can tell by the pen, which is green, and the handwriting, which is loopy) has commented on people throughout the book, mostly boys (*My future husband*; *Mama's boy*; *Hubba, hubba*).

Denise.

Her picture is near the end of the section, and I have to stop myself from laughing out loud. Everyone else has polite little smiles, but Denise looks like she just told a bad joke — she's smiling big as a Muppet, with all her teeth showing. I can't get over how young she looks. Everything is a little too big on her face, as if she hasn't quite grown into it yet. And her hair looks like it's been assisted by both a curling and crimping iron. I'm not even sure what you would call that style other than maybe "the cloud."

The person with the green pen also drew a box around the picture and added little rays, like the ones children draw around suns. There's a comment beside it: *The coolest person I have ever met!*

Yep. The person with the green pen was definitely a teenage Denise.

There is knock at the door. I slam the yearbook shut and slip it under my pillow.

"Come in."

The door opens and Doug is there, holding Suzy's leash.

"Are you ready? It's go time!"

Ever since the engagement, Doug has asked me to "tag along" when he walks his dog, Suzy. I'm not much of a dog person, and I'm definitely not a Suzy person. I have never quite forgiven her for running away from me last spring, even though it did lead to one of the more interesting moments of my life: kissing Michael. I still blush just thinking about it.

Doug never uses the word "bonding," but it's clear that these walks are for us to get to know each other. Now that he is moving in permanently, it seems like a good idea. If I didn't go, I'm sure my mother would find a horrible task for me to do, like fishing hairballs from the drain pipe in the Hair Emporium. Even half an hour with Doug and his hairball of a dog is better than that.

Luckily Doug is a talker, so there are never any awkward moments.

"So, C-Bot, you haven't said a word about me moving in."

As part of our bonding process, Doug is constantly coming up with new nicknames for me. Some are better than others.

I can feel him looking at me, waiting for a response. Even though they've been engaged for more than a week, Doug hasn't asked me how I feel about it yet. I knew it was only a matter of time before the questions came. Doug can't help himself when it comes to talking things out.

I keep my eyes on the dog, who is basically skipping along the sidewalk, her nose to the cement, sniffing out who knows what. Unlike the other dogs we pass, she seems incapable of walking in a straight line, preferring to zigzag around, depending on what interesting smells she can find.

"I think it's good," I say to him, still looking at Suzy.

"You can be honest with me. I know it's a big change."

"I know. We've never had a pet before," I say.

Doug laughs. He thinks I'm being funny. "It's nothing. You'll love it."

Just then Suzy spots a single fallen leaf, drops to her haunches and starts barking at it. I'm not so sure I *will* love living with such a dumb dog.

Doug goes on, "Suzy will be a change, that's for sure, but I was talking about me moving in. How do you feel about that?"

I wonder if this is how it's going to be now: Doug asking me questions about my feelings while we walk his dog. I feel like we're on a family sitcom, and this is the part where the father and daughter have a heart-to-heart. Only Doug is not my father, and I hate heart-to-hearts.

If this is going to be our new thing, then it is an unfortunate side effect of his moving in. I don't like to talk things out; I do enough of that with Mattie. I don't need another amateur psychiatrist in my life.

Nor do I need a dog, come to think of it.

"I'm okay with it. I'm still sort of . . . processing the information."

Processing the information? Now I sound like Mattie.

Inside, I'm cringing, but Doug is nodding.

"Totally. I get that. It's going to take some time. That's

why we thought I'd move in in stages," he explains, sounding suspiciously like my mother. It hits me that they probably discussed how they would approach me, mapping out all my possible reactions and deciding how they'd respond.

This is something they will do, now. They will have secret conversations to discuss things like allowance and curfew and whether or not I am being too mouthy. They will be Team Parent and I will be all alone. There is no one on my side. Except for maybe the dog.

Suzy bounces up, snapping her jaws at a moth. Even the moth, the laziest and dopiest of insects, gets away. This doesn't seem to bother Suzy. She still runs over to Doug, elated, as if she had caught it. Doug leans down and roughs up her doggy bangs, jabbering away to her in baby talk.

Who am I kidding? That dog is not on my team. It's just me against Team Parent and their sweet-natured, if a little slow, mascot Suzy.

Research Day

Because Mattie is leaving for camp soon, we are trying to spend as much time together as possible. She even comes over just to hang out while I cover the phone for the Hair Emporium. Mattie loves it, especially when I let her answer the phone and make appointments. She's so good at it: very professional and friendly.

Today I got roped into packing the last of the boxes that are headed to the Salvation Army. With Mattie around, I barely have to do any of the actual work. She's happy to organize, and I do my best to add my two cents from the bed, flipping through the yearbooks.

"Clarissa, you aren't being very helpful."

"Sorry, you're just doing such a good job."

Mattie tosses an old tuque at my head. "Yeah, right. What are you doing? Are those yearbooks?"

"Yeah, they're my mom's."

Mattie squeals, abandons her organizing and steps through piles of winter clothes to sit on the bed next to me. "Let's go through them!"

I'm happy to pore over them again. We go through the yearbooks one by one, laughing at the hairstyles and wondering over all the mysterious notes.

"Your mom was so pretty," Mattie says. "My mom had these

horrible glasses in high school. You could barely see her face!"

"Do you want to see my dad?"

Mattie draws her breath in sharply. "Are you serious? They went to high school together?"

"Yep."

"Show me."

I find the grade eleven yearbook and flip to the prom picture. "That's him."

Mattie takes the book from me, sets it on her lap and stares at it for a few moments before declaring, "He's handsome. Don't you think so? I would date him."

I take the yearbook back, snapping it shut. "Ew, don't be gross!"

I should have known Mattie would take what could have been a nice moment and make it all about boys.

"I'm not — I'm giving him a compliment! Do you ever wonder about him?"

"Not really. A few times, maybe. But lately I've been thinking about him more."

"And you've never spoken to him?"

"Never."

Mattie shakes her head. "I can't believe it. It's like something out of a movie. Have you ever looked him up online?"

"No."

"Really? Why not?"

I'm embarrassed to admit that even though I've considered it in the past, I always chickened out. "It didn't seem like such a big deal before."

Mattie's eyes wander over to the computer. "Want to look him up now?"

Now that the seed has been planted, I do want to look him up. "Okay, but let me close the door first."

Mattie frowns. "Why?"

"Just in case my mom comes up and wants to know what we're doing."

"Why would she care? He's your dad. It's not illegal to Google your own father," Mattie says.

"I know, but she'd probably overreact. She'd think it was this big deal." I roll my eyes, as if to say "mothers, what can you do?" even though my heartbeat is speeding up and my skin is itching, which is what happens to me when I'm excited or anxious. This is, in fact, a huge deal. I've never done anything other than ask Denise a few questions about Bill before. I'm in completely new territory here.

Mattie sits at my computer, and I sit on the bed behind her. It feels safer to let her do the typing, as if I'm just an innocent bystander and have nothing to do with it.

"What's his name?"

"Bill Davies. I don't know his middle name."

"Do you think he goes by Bill or William?"

"I don't know."

"Let's look up William Davies first."

Over three million results pop up. This is going to be more difficult than I thought.

"We have to narrow it somehow," Mattie says.

"He lives in Vancouver. Maybe type in 'Bill Davies, Vancouver.'"

Mattie types the words in as requested. Still way too many hits to go through, but definitely less than three million. The first three entries that pop up are a LinkedIn profile, an obituary and a movie database listing for an actor.

"Which one should we check first?"

"Go to the actor."

"Good idea. Maybe you get your love of acting from him," Mattie says, optimistic as ever.

But Bill Davies the actor turns out to be a twenty-six-year-old black man.

"Obviously not. Try the LinkedIn profile."

That also ends up being a bust. The Bill Davies listed there is too old and doesn't look a thing like my father does in his high school photos.

"Remember that people change," Mattie points out.

"That man's face is an entirely different shape, he has red hair and he's at least ten years too old."

Mattie sighs. "I know. I'm just trying to be positive. Do you want me to check the obituary?"

I hesitate. Even if I've never met him, I'm not sure I want to find out whether or not my father is dead just yet. I take a deep breath, gripping the back of the computer chair so hard my knuckles turn bone white. "Okay. Let's do it."

According to the obituary, the Bill Davies who died last Saturday was eighty-four years old and left behind two children and six grandkids in Surrey, B.C. I let out a big sigh.

"That's a relief," Mattie says. "Do you know anything else about him?"

"I think Denise said he worked in sales."

So Mattie types in *"Bill Davies" Vancouver, sales.* Two lawyers, a photographer and a police report pop-up. A quick check proves that none of these men are the right Bill, either.

"This is impossible," I sigh. "There are too many Bill Davieses in the world."

"Don't give up so quickly!"

"What's the point? What am I going to do, email him?"

Mattie thinks about it for a moment. "Maybe. Or maybe

you can just read about him and move on."

"What do you mean, move on? It's not like he's holding me back. I barely think about him. It's just these stupid yearbooks."

"Maybe . . . " Mattie begins, then she trails off.

"Maybe what?"

"Or maybe the yearbooks are a sign."

"What kind of sign?"

"A sign that you are meant to look him up. Why else would you find them now? They've been in your house forever."

"That's crazy. They turned up because we were cleaning."

"Maybe, maybe not. Let's try Facebook."

Next Mattie signs into Facebook and searches for his name. Not surprisingly, there are tons of Bill Davies from all over the world. It's hard to tell from the little profile pictures that pop up, but none of them look anything like the picture in the yearbook.

"Maybe he doesn't like the internet," Mattie says. "My Aunt Karen moved to Vancouver and now she lives on an organic farm that uses solar power to heat the water. She hates cell phones and microwaves because she thinks they give you cancer. Maybe your dad is one of those back-to-the-earth types."

"I doubt it. The way Denise described him, he doesn't seem like the kind of person who goes for solar power and electric cars and all that."

Mattie sighs, crestfallen. "I'm sorry this was so useless."

"It's not your fault. Like you said, maybe this is a sign. Only this time the sign is telling me to forget it."

Mattie frowns. "That's the most depressing sign I've ever heard of."

Truth be told, my spirits have dipped a little low, too. A big part of me was looking forward to learning about Bill Davies. But looking for him online was like looking for a needle in a haystack, only the haystack was the internet — the biggest haystack in the world.

"Can't you just ask your mom?"

I shake my head. "No way. I told you, she'd read into it and take it too seriously."

Mattie wasn't finished. "But she must have some way to contact him. Maybe she's been waiting all these years for you to ask, letting you come to her in your own time."

"You read too many books," I say.

"Maybe you should read *more* books," Mattie says, just the slightest bit of sass in her voice.

"Why should I? It's summer."

Mattie rolls her eyes, but laughs. "You never know unless you ask," she says.

"Trust me, I know. She'd completely freak out," I say.

Move-in Day

For the past two weeks, whenever he dropped by, Doug brought a box or two over with him. The house is like an obstacle course: boxes in the living room, boxes stacked in the hall outside the master bedroom — there are even a few boxes in the bathroom beside the toilet. I have no desire to open these.

But today Doug has brought over the final load of boxes and the most significant piece of baggage: Suzy. For such a little dog she sure comes with a lot of stuff. Along with her stainless steel bowls and enormous potato-sack sized bags of food, she has a travel crate, a regular crate, a sleeping pillow, a variety of very worn blankets and an entire box of toys. I don't mean a shoebox; I mean a box that originally held a microwave. It's possible that Suzy has more toys than I ever did.

Having Suzy around might be the weirdest part about Doug moving in. I've gotten used to seeing him at the dinner table or watching TV on the couch with my mom, but Suzy will be a new fixture in our everyday lives. Doug will be at work for part of the day, so I won't really see him much more than I used to before he moved in. But now Suzy will always be around, sniffing at our heels, trying to eat our shoes and crying if we don't give her enough attention.

Tonight my mother puts her foot down for the first time since the move-in started. She does not want Suzy to sleep in their room.

"She's a cutie, but I don't need to vacuum dog hair off my comforter every day," she says.

Doug appears to take the news quite hard. He looks truly sombre, as if imagining the moment he has to break the news to Suzy. Eventually, he agrees. Annie Delaney is a hard woman to argue with.

"For now, let's confine her to the kitchen at night," Doug says sadly. "It's probably better if she gets used to the house one room at a time."

Suzy has been to our house plenty of times, so she doesn't seem to get that something is up until Doug traps her in the kitchen with a complicated series of baby gates. At first she thinks it's a game, jumping around in circles and growling at us through the gate.

"That sounds threatening," I say, taking a step back toward my room. "Are you sure that gate will hold?"

"She's just playing," Doug insists.

"But what if she decides that I'm responsible for locking her up and manages to get out in the middle of the night, hunting me down in my sleep?"

"She's a dog, not a tiger, Clarissa."

She may be a dog, but right now she's growling like a tiger. But neither Doug nor Mom seems worried by her aggressive behaviour.

As we head to our rooms, the growling turns to whining and then barking in loud, evenly spaced barks. It sounds like she's sending out some kind of doggy distress signal. Any minute now other dogs, from all over town, are going to start barking in response.

"Is she going to do that all night?" I ask.

"Probably not," Doug says.

"Probably not?" I repeat.

"Just ignore her."

Easier said than done. Suzy has more stamina than I thought possible, and after fifteen straight minutes of her sounding the doggy alarm, I'm ready to climb out the window and go sleep at Benji's.

Doug yells at her from the bedroom, "Suzy-Q! Quiet down, now! Atta girl."

Hearing Doug's voice does nothing to calm Suzy down. Instead, it encourages her to change tactics. Now she's whining, a sound so pitiful that it even manages to pull on my heartstrings. I may not be the biggest Suzy fan, but I'm not cruel. I know it must be lonely being cooped up in a strange place, especially for a dog that used to sleep at the feet of her one and only master.

From the other bedroom, I hear the bed creak and the door open. Then Mom's voice rings loud and clear into the hallway. "Don't. You're only showing her that if she whines, you'll come running."

Burn, Doug. You just got told. I smile into my pillow, even though Suzy has gone back to barking, and it's not clear if we will ever sleep in peace again. It's nice to know that Mom still knows how to rule the roost. To myself, I think, Clarissa 1, Suzy 0.

But at three o'clock in the morning, after I'm rudely awakened by round two of Suzy's protest, I change that score to Clarissa 1, Suzy 1.

This is going to be even more difficult than I imagined.

A Long, Boring Day

Dear Clarissa,

My cabin is singing in the talent show and Wicker is teaching us this AMAZING four part harmony and people are really going to be blown away. Wicker is by far the best counsellor I have ever had. You would really like her, Clarissa. She's kind of tough and so fun — just like you! Plus, she plays guitar and designs tattoos and is the best archery teacher in the world. It's like taking lessons from Katniss Everdeen!!! I almost got a bull's eye, although you should see all the bruises I have on my arms from archery. So not pretty!

I've made a big decision. I'm going to break up with Andrew. I've been thinking about it for a long time, and even though he is really sweet and smart, the connection just isn't there, not like it is with you and Michael (are you guys official yet?!?!). He's only written me once, and all he talked about was what he had for dinner and the games he was working on at computer camp. He never said one romantic thing. I know he's really shy, but I have decided I need a boy who is not afraid to show his emo-

tions. Besides, there are going to be so many other boys at Sir John A., and I want to keep my options open. I'm too young to settle down! So now you know. By the time I come home it will be over. I would much rather do it in person, but that's not really possible, so I'm going to compose a heartfelt, sensitive letter. Wicker has broken up with lots of boys so she's going to help me.

Have you given any thought about coming to camp next year? I really think you would love it if you just gave it a chance. It's not one of those hard-core camps where you cook your own food every night over a campfire and sleep in tents. We have cabins and bunk beds and a kitchen that makes AMAZING mac & cheese. Please think about it, Clarissa. I love camp, but I miss you and I know we would have such a great time together! And then you could meet Wicker!

Say hello to your mom and tell her I'm going to need major highlights when I get back! You should see how the sun has wrecked my hair! Also say hi to Benji and Charity for me and be sure to give Michael a big kiss (ha-ha!). You can even say it's from me, you big chicken!

I miss you, but only on days that end in y. (Ha! Get it?! Wicker taught me that!)

XOXOXO

Mattie

I fold Mattie's letter and leave it on the coffee table. I will add it to my collection later. She is a dutiful pen pal, writing two times a week, sometimes even more.

I look forward to her letters. I've already read this one about fifteen times since it arrived on Thursday. Sadly, walking to the mailbox after lunch has become the highlight of my day. I hate to admit it, but I'm bored. It feels wrong to not take advantage of summer, but there's only so much I can do on my own. Benji is fully occupied with drama camp, which seem to be taking up some of his evenings, too. In past summers, whenever things got dull, at least we were bored together. Being bored on your own is a totally different story.

I keep finding myself hanging around the Hair Emporium out of sheer desperation.

"What's wrong with you?" Denise asks, barely looking up from her magazine. "You're spoiling the lovely, peaceful ambiance with your sulking."

Oh right, and her snapping her gum and tapping the toes of her shoes against the metal bar of the stylist chair isn't?

"I'm bored."

Denise sighs. "Must be nice to be young and have the luxury of being bored. These days I don't have time to eat, let alone get bored."

"And yet you manage to make time to drop by here every day," I point out.

Denise ignores me and continues ranting. "Do you know how much time I've spent in the car this week? Twenty hours. That's almost a full day! These sales calls are going to be the death of me. If I don't drop dead from exhaustion, I'll probably die in a head-on collision."

Mom makes a supportive murmuring noise and folds another strand of Denise's red hair up in a little foil package.

"Don't you think you're being a little paranoid?" I ask.

"Think about it: I spend more time in a car than anyone I know. Odds are if anyone's going to get in an accident, it's me. I'm not being paranoid; I'm just considering the numbers."

"Didn't you fail grade ten math?"

Mom gives me a warning look that Denise can't see. "Why don't you give Benji a call?" she suggests.

"He has drama."

"It's Saturday; I thought drama camp was just weekdays," Mom says.

"He's decided to help out with the little kids," I grumble, still not quite believing it.

When Benji told me he'd decided to volunteer with the Kiddie Camp, I was completely shocked. Benji has never shown any interest in kids before.

"But why?" I'd asked.

"It's good practice."

"Practice for what? It's not like you get to act! You're basically babysitting for free!"

"No, but I get to help out backstage and with costuming. And Charity says any time spent with Dean, the director, is valuable. Did I tell you that he goes to theatre school? He had to audition to get in. They only take, like, ten people a year!"

I knew then that he was a lost cause. Benji takes everything Charity says to be the final word. If *she* told him it was a good idea, I'd never be able to change his mind.

"That Benji. What a sweetie," Denise says now. "That kid is going places, just you wait."

I've had about enough Denise for one day. I stuff the magazine I've been idly flipping through into the rack and stomp up the stairs, making as much noise as I can.

"Where are you going?" Mom asks.

"Anywhere but here," I say. "The smell of hair dye is making me nauseous."

"Come back, kiddo! I want to talk to you about dresses," Denise calls after me.

Fat chance.

It's after four. Surely Benji is back from babysitting future *Toddlers in Tiaras* contestants.

But when I call him, his line flips right over to voicemail, which means someone is on the phone. The Dentonator isn't a phone person, so it can only be Benji. I wait a few more minutes and try again, only to hear a click and the voicemail message, like before.

Next door, the lights are on in the Dentons' house, but everything is shut up tight because of the Dentonator's obsession with air conditioning. Walking into Benji's house in the summer is like walking into the frozen foods aisle at the grocery store. Before long your teeth are chattering and goosebumps have exploded all over your arms.

I decide to head over to put in some face-time. The Dentonator answers the door, and cold, refrigerated air leaks out onto the porch. At first it's kind of nice, like your first gulp of cold water, but then I start to shiver a little.

"Hi, Mr. D. Is Benji around?"

Benji's bulk of a dad points a thumb over his shoulder. "He's here, on the phone. Tying up the line, again."

Again? How many nights does Benji spend on the phone? Who could he possibly be talking to? I'm the one he calls most of the time, and we haven't talked on the phone for a while.

"Who's he talking to?"

"Don't know for sure. Probably one of those dramarama people." The Dentonator has not yet fully embraced Benji's new-found passion for theatre. I think the poor guy was still holding out for the day Benji decided he did, in fact, like hockey. Adults can be seriously delusional.

"Charity?" I ask, feeling a little twinge of not-quite jealousy. After all, Charity and I are friends now, even if she is older, prettier and generally better at life than I am.

"Could be. I don't know. Do you want to come in and wait? It's a sweatbox out there."

"No, thanks." I'd rather sweat to death than sit on a couch-Popsicle making small talk with the Dentonator. "Can you tell him to call me when he's off the phone?"

"Will do."

I go home to wait for Benji's call. Doug is doing the lunch dishes. I have to admit, Doug is learning the ropes pretty quickly. He has learned, for example, that Annie Delaney will not tolerate dirty dishes in the sink. Still, the sight of him wearing yellow rubber gloves and singing under his breath stops me in my tracks. I wonder if I'll ever get used to seeing him doing normal house things.

"Hey there, Clarissa. Shouldn't you be out living it up with your pals?"

"They've all deserted me to die of boredom."

"Well, that will never do. Give me half an hour to finish up here and shower, then we can take Suzy-Q for her walk."

"Actually, I'm waiting for Benji to call. We were going to hang out."

"Tell you what, if he doesn't call before walk time, you're more than welcome to join us."

I'm so bored, I agree to this plan. Then I head downstairs to watch TV while I wait for Benji to call. I flip through channels, not really watching anything.

It feels like the whole world has better things to do, except me. Hurry up, Benji! I concentrate on sending him get-off-the-phone vibes. I don't really believe in things like that, but freaky coincidental things used to happen to us all the time. Like, I'd pick up the phone to call him and there would be no dial tone, only dead air. After a second a voice would say hello, and it would be Benji on the other end, calling me. That hasn't happened in a while. We don't see each other as often as we used to, so maybe the connection has broken. Or not broken, but worn thin over time, like an old rope on a tetherball.

Half an hour later, Doug is standing at the back door with Suzy tugging at her leash.

"Any word from Sir Benjamin?" he calls down the stairs.

"No," I admit.

"Well, Suzy and I would love the pleasure of your company."

"Just a second." I call Benji one more time, only to be thwarted by the voicemail once more. I slam the receiver in the cradle. Seriously, who is he having half-hour conversations with?

"Dog train is leaving the station," Doug says.

"I'm coming, I'm coming."

"So what's up with you and Benji?" Doug asks as we hit the sidewalk.

"He's obsessed with drama camp."

"That's understandable. He's found his passion."

"I know. It's just that, usually, we spend all summer together. We go on these missions . . ." I trail off, thinking about the things Benji and I used to do. They'd probably sound stupid to Doug.

"I like the sound of missions," Doug says. "Give me an example."

"Well, one summer we vowed to watch every single Judy Garland movie we could find in the library."

Doug looks confused. "Judy Garland?" he asks.

"The actress? She played Dorothy in *The Wizard of Oz*?"

41

Can he seriously not know who she is?

"Oh, *her*. That's pretty old school."

"She made a lot of movies," I say. "Most of them musical. Anyway, that was 'Mission: Judy!' And one summer we took the swept-up old hair from the Hair Emporium and left handfuls of it in parks around town so that birds could make nests with it. Then we spent the rest of the summer hunting for nests with human hair in them. We used these old binoculars someone left on the side of the road. They worked fine, but the strap was broken and one of the lenses was cracked."

"That's totally gross and fascinating," Doug says.

"You'd better get used to having dead hair around if you're going to live with us," I say.

"I'll manage. Did you find any nests?"

"We found two. It was hard to know for sure if the hair was *our* hair, but if we saw a nest with hair woven into it we just claimed it as our own."

"That seems fair. Was this last year?"

"No, 'Mission: Birdnest' was a while ago. Last year we made it our mission to bike down every street in town."

"How long did that take you?"

"Not very long. Halfway through, Benji got the idea that we should pose with every street sign, but we didn't want to go back and get pictures of the streets we'd already been to, so we're missing a bunch."

I leave out the part about how we also tried not to be seen, like spies, which meant a lot of ducking behind cars and hiding behind bushes. It seems kind of stupid now, but it made us laugh really hard then.

"As a fitness professional, I approve of your cycling adventures."

"Benji made a scrapbook. It's called 'Mission: Biketown.' We wrote notes in it and everything. He'd probably show it to you if you asked."

"I'd love to take a look-see, as long as you don't mind. Sounds like these missions are a private Benji and Clarissa operation."

Talking about the missions makes me feel a little sad. Summer started weeks ago, and neither of us has so much as mentioned this year's mission. We've done lots of stuff together, like barbeques, movies, even a few bike rides, but it feels different, less special. For one thing, there's almost always someone else with us: Mattie or Charity or some of Benji's drama friends. Doug is right; the missions were always something just the two of us did. Maybe we've grown out of them.

The thought makes my heart ache, like it's grown too big for its space in my chest.

An Early Day

The Hair Emporium opens at nine every morning, but sometimes Mom will make an exception. It's not unusual to hear voices from the salon as early as eight, or sometimes seven-thirty, but it is unusual when one of those voices is Benji's. In fact, when I stumble to the bathroom at 8:05 in the morning, I'm not even sure that it's him I hear giggling away with my mother in the basement. I stand outside the bathroom door, straining to make out their voices.

I'd intended to go back to bed and sleep for at least another hour, but now my curiosity is waking me up, like a big cup of coffee — which, despite my status as a fourteen-year-old young adult about to enter high school, I am still not allowed to drink.

I manage to make it through the kitchen and down the stairs to the salon without tripping over my clumsy, sleepy feet. Sure enough, there's Benji sitting in one of the big red leather chairs, flowered cape Velcroed around his neck, Mom running her little black comb through his wet hair, snipping away.

"Benji? What are you doing here?"

Mom smiles, but Benji looks guilty, like he's been caught doing something he shouldn't.

"Good morning to you, too, Clarissa," Mom says. She is

44

a morning person and doesn't understand how it can take some people (like me, for example) a little more time to warm up to the idea of being awake. She pats the empty chair next to her. Obediently, I head over, pausing to spritz my face with the water spray bottle Mom uses to keep people's hair damp. I've only been up for five minutes and already it's too hot to function. The cool mist helps a little. I offer to spritz Benji's face.

"No thanks," he says.

"Didn't you just get a haircut?"

"It's quite common for men to get trims more frequently than women," Mom interjects.

Benji's hair is now quite short at the back and longer in the front. Before his hair just existed, void of any particular style. It was merely something that grew out of his head and occasionally needed to be brushed.

"That's not just a trim; you're styling it."

"That is what I do," Mom says brightly, then continues to run her comb through Benji's hair, snipping along an invisible line only she can see.

"Is it for your camp play?" I ask.

"It's not exactly a play; it's a showcase of famous numbers from musicals throughout time," Benji reminds me.

"Whatever. What I mean is, are you getting your hair styled because you're playing a character who needs a cool haircut?"

"Like in *West Side Story*?"

I frown. A singing and dancing gang member is not exactly what I meant by cool.

"Sure, like in *West Side Story*."

"No, Dean says we don't need to look the part; we just need to embody it."

"Right. So if it isn't for the showcase, what's with the crazy cut?"

Mom clucks her tongue. "You don't need a reason to get a haircut, Clarissa! Half my business is people who decide they want a change on the spur of the moment." She shakes her head in mock disappointment. "And to think you're my own flesh and blood."

Maybe some people don't need a reason, but Benji always gets his hair cut the first Saturday morning of every month. He's never had so much as a trim in between visits before.

"Besides, you're starting high school in a few weeks. It's the perfect time for something different. New school, new look. Right, Benji?" Mom squeezes his shoulders and smiles at him in the mirror, making full use of her dimples.

Benji smiles back. "I wanted something cooler," he admits.

"Since when do you care about cool?" I demand.

"Quiet, please. I must have my client's full attention for the big reveal." Mom whips the cape from Benji's shoulders and brushes the back of his neck with her big fluffy brush, dusting away any stray hairs. "Ready to check out the new you?"

"Ready."

She takes out a hand mirror with a red handle and holds it at just the right spot so Benji can check out his new 'do in the mirror. He pats his hair carefully, as if it might fall out or disappear if he presses too hard.

"Good?" Mom asks.

Benji grins. "Good," he agrees. Then he hops off the chair and takes out a twenty-dollar bill, which Mom waves off.

"Don't be silly, your cuts are always on the house."

"Are you sure?" Benji says.

"Absolutely."

I resist rolling my eyes. Benji has been trying to pay for his haircuts since the day his dad sent him wandering in here with hair in his eyes and a twenty-dollar bill balled up in his seven-year-old fist. Mom always refuses his money, but they go through the whole charade every time.

Now that the cape is gone, I can see his whole outfit: his good black jeans and what looks like a new plaid shirt worn open over his cast shirt from *The Wizard of Oz*. The collar of the plaid shirt is perfectly stiff, and I can still see the crease from where it was folded over a square of cardboard in the store. I am dumbfounded. Thought went into that outfit. Benji looks, well, styled.

"Is that shirt new?"

"I got it on the weekend. It's for school."

"And you're wearing it to rehearsal?"

Benji looks down at his new shirt, running his hands over the black and teal squares. "Why not? Don't you like it?"

"I thought you were supposed to wear all black." I distinctly remember a conversation in which Benji talked about buying "blacks" that he could "move in" for rehearsal. I remember it because I wanted to know what the difference was between all-black and all-grey clothes when it came to movement, and he couldn't answer the question.

"Dean says we can wear whatever we want as long as we can move in it."

Stiff jeans and a new shirt don't seem all that flexible to me, but what do I know? "Don't you spend all your time rolling around on the floor and getting into character? Won't it get wrecked?"

"Since when did you become the fashion police?" Mom

asks. "Ignore her, Benji. I think you look great. Like the Biebs."

"*Mom*, do *not* say 'The Biebs.'"

Now Benji looks worried. "Does it look like I'm trying too hard? Tell me the truth."

I want to ask, trying too hard for what? Who does he have to impress at drama camp? But he looks worried, and I hate when Benji looks worried, so I say, "No, you look good. Just . . . different."

Which is the truth. The hair, the outfit, the whole thing looks so polished, so put together. Who is this cool new person, I think. And then Benji smiles and he's him again.

"Different is good," he says.

"I guess," I say, not convinced.

"I should go! Bye, Annie, thanks for the cut. See you later Clarissa."

"Later."

Mom watches him go. When he's out of earshot she presses a hand to her heart and sighs. "Bless him. He used to be such a shy little thing and now look at him!"

I roll my eyes. "I'm going back to bed now," I say.

Lazy Day

Mom is busy all day with clients, and Doug is at work. I have nothing but time to study the yearbooks in greater depth.

I settle into the big lounge chair on the back porch with a glass that is full of one-third lemonade, one-third ice tea and one-third ice cubes. All of my hair is stuffed up in one of Mom's floppy hats. I feel a little ridiculous, but convince myself there is no one around to see me, and besides, I don't want to be burned in all of the wedding pictures.

The best part of a yearbook is the autograph section. There are two pages set aside for autographs in the back, but my mom was so popular people wrote on the endpapers and in the margins of some of the photo pages, too. Most of the messages are pretty standard (*Have a great year!*) or fall under the you-had-to-be-there category (*Don't let the Purpleman get you down!*).

It is clear Mom had lots of fans, judging from the things some people wrote, everything from mushy (*You are such an inspiration and I know you're gonna do amazing things*) to creepy (*You're so awesome! I want to be you!*).

I linger over all the mysterious autographs and wonder what they mean. Like who or what is "The Purpleman"? Three different people reference him in their messages. It has to mean something, but what?

Bill (it feels weird to call him my father) took over a whole page. At the top of the page, the words *THIS PAGE BELONGS TO BILL DAVIES* are written in block letters. A single message, written in large scraggly letters, fills the entire page, so different from the rest of the autograph pages with their patchwork of cramped messages.

It says, *To my Queen, let's run away and find another kingdom to rule. This place isn't good enough for someone so beautiful and charmeing . . . me! Ha-ha, just kidding, you know I meant you. Everyone in this school looks at you and thinks, Damn, that Bill is lucky! But no one knows it more than me. Can't wait for summer when we can spend every day together. The world is our oyster, babe, so let's get shucking!"*

I blush reading it, not because of how cheesy it is or the bad pun or because he spelled charming wrong, but because it feels like I've snooped into someone's diary or private love letters. And not just anyone's, but my own parents'.

In the Activity Photos section, I discover that Annie Delaney and Bill Davies were voted cutest couple that year. In the picture, they are posing under an arch wrapped in voluminous clouds of tulle. They must be at a big dance of some kind, like prom. They stand close to each other, almost cheek-to-cheek. Bill is wearing a bulky leather jacket over a suit with his collar open; his hair is messy and huge sunglasses are perched on his nose. He is staring down the camera like a rebel in an old movie.

Mom is wearing a shiny blue dress with rhinestoned straps and a skirt that has about fifteen layers of satin ruffles. She is holding a pair of sunglasses on her head as if they are about to fall off, laughing at Bill mugging away for the camera.

They look fun, like the kind of people who don't take things like prom photos too seriously but manage to take an awesome picture anyway. I try to find traces of my own face in Bill's features, but the picture is too small and half his face is obscured by sunglasses. I wish I had the original photograph. I wonder what's happened to it after all these years?

The phone rings, rudely interrupting my lovely afternoon. My only job during the summer is to answer the phone for my mother. We agreed I wouldn't have to sit at the little desk in the salon all day, as long as I got up to answer the phone. She will most definitely kill me if I can't keep up my end of the bargain, so I put down my iced lemon-tea and run for it before the voicemail kicks in.

"Good afternoon, Hair Emporium."

"Clarissa? It's me. Michael."

Michael still feels the need to introduce himself, even though I know perfectly well who is on the other end of the line.

"Hey."

"Are you coming to the game tonight?"

"Sure. If you want me to."

"Yeah, that'd be great. I mean, if you want to."

Michael and I often have frustratingly polite conversations like this.

"Of course! What time?"

"Seven. We're playing at the school again, on the north diamond."

He means our soon-to-be-old school, Ferndale, and the north diamond is the one furthest from the building.

"Okay! See you there!"

"See you."

Tonight feels very far away. I miss my friends. Alone time is seriously overrated.

Game Day

Baseball is pretty boring. No one ever seems to hit the ball, and when they do, it never goes far. If anyone gets two bases on a single hit it's a miracle. Michael turns really red when he's playing. I wonder if it's nerves or me. I hope that a little bit of it is because of me.

One thing that's nice about coming to these games is I can watch Michael without anyone accusing me of staring at him. At a game you're supposed to watch the player. Plus, behind my sunglasses, no one can tell that I watch Michael even when he's not at bat. It's the perfect set-up.

Michael's father comes to the games, but he sits with some other dads and they talk the whole time, explaining all the coach's decisions and comparing their sons' batting averages. They clap for each other's sons and share food. Chips mostly, but sometimes mixed nuts.

"Clarissa! Is that you?" Mrs. Greenblat doesn't come very often, but when she does, she brings all three of Michael's brothers and insists we sit together.

I smile and wave as she makes her way up the bleachers, Theo in her arms and David and Solly stomping along behind. David is singing at the top of his lungs.

"Be a dear and take Theo for a second? David's laces are untied again. I don't want him falling to his death."

Mrs. Greenblat hands me Theo, who is not quite two, as if he is nothing more than a purse. I don't really know how to hold him, so I plunk him on my lap, facing the game, and cross my arms around his middle like a big human seatbelt. Mrs. Greenblat is under the mistaken impression that I am one of those girls who babysits and wants nothing more than to make faces at toddlers and ask them silly questions (Does baby like his tummy tickled? Who's a silly boy?). No wonder it takes kids so long to learn to talk. No one ever asks them anything interesting.

Luckily, Theo is a pretty calm baby, who doesn't sense how uncomfortable I am, and is happy to sit on my lap and squeal at the baseball game.

"There you go. Now you can run as much as you like. If you trip, it won't be because of those laces."

With a war cry that seems too big for such a little kid (David is five, and a scrawny five at that), David jumps off the bleachers, falls, then gets up and runs for the trees that border the playground.

"Be careful, David," Mrs. Greenblat calls after him. "Stay where I can see you and don't cross the street." For someone who didn't want her son to trip on his shoelaces, Mrs. Greenblat doesn't seem all that concerned about David jumping off bleachers.

"Clarissa, do you want to see my book?" Solly asks.

"Sure!" I say. Anything is better than this baseball game, which is still 0–0 despite being in what feels like the eighteenth inning. Solly is almost nine and is my favourite of Michael's brothers, mostly because he doesn't wear a diaper (Theo) or run around yelling like a maniac (David). He can quote entire scenes from movies, and he memorizes whole pages out of his beloved fact books. You have to admire a kid like that.

"Look, this is the intestinal system. Here's where the food goes. Then it becomes bile, and then we poop it out. See how the poop is in the toilet there?" Solly points to an illustration of a gigantic turd, steaming in a toilet. Cripes.

Mrs. Greenblat laughs and whisks the book away from Solly, stashing it in her gigantic purse. "Sorry, Clarissa. I should have warned you. This is Solly's new favourite book. We think it means he's going to grow up and be a doctor someday."

I try to laugh, but the illustration of food decomposing in a green stew of bile — and the suspicious smell that is coming from baby Theo — makes it extremely difficult.

Michael's mom talks through the whole baseball game, but she rarely mentions the game itself. She's nice and everything, but sometimes I don't know what to say. When I told my mom that sometimes Mrs. Greenblat comes, she said it was probably a real treat for her to get out of the house and talk to another woman.

"You mean me?" I scoffed.

"Yes, you."

"Shouldn't she have friends her own age?"

"I think it's nice of you. Plus you might learn a thing or two."

"About what, baby talk?"

"You never know when that will come in handy," Denise threw in, slyly.

"Not likely," I mumbled, but then I caught myself. I'm fourteen. Mom was only eighteen when she had me, which means she was pregnant at seventeen. Even now, the thought sends monster shivers down my spine. It's just one more reminder of how high school is a different beast and everything is about to change. Again.

I keep thinking Mrs. Greenblat is going to take Theo from me. He's getting heavy and my legs are starting to fall asleep. Do diapers leak? I shift him as well as I can, hoping she'll notice, but no such luck. Instead, she goes into a marathon rant about how hyperactivity is a direct result of too much sugar and not enough physical activity. She's saying something about alternate ways to channel excess energy when I see him: a man, watching the game and fooling around on a cell phone at the same time.

I spend a lot of time people watching during these games. It gives me something to do when Michael is on the bench. After a while you start to recognize people, or at least the people they're sitting with. This man has never come before, but there is something familiar about him. His shoulders are hunched and bony and his long legs look funny and almost painful, the way they are bent to accommodate the bleachers, which are clearly not meant for long legs. He has a hat on, but his hair curls around the edges.

I'm staring so hard that when he takes his hat off and rubs his head, I think it must be because he can feel me staring at him. Like I'm burning the back of his neck with my eyes. He looks over his shoulder and I can see him full on for the first time. My heart stops, or maybe it's just my breathing. Whatever it is, I must have made a noise, because Mrs. Greenblat puts her hand on my shoulder and asks if I'm okay.

I'm unable to answer. How can I, when barely 3 metres away from me, after all this time, is my father?

Unbelievable Day

Time doesn't stop, exactly: it feels more like I have laser focus, and everything that's not him goes blurry. I take my sunglasses off with one hand, still holding onto Theo with the other, so I can get a better look. My heart feels like it's pumping in my throat, and I have to swallow a few times before I can speak.

"I wonder who that is," I say as casually as possible, nodding at him. "I've never seen him before."

Mrs. Greenblat squints at the man who may be my father. "No idea. But I don't think he's one of the fathers. Maybe he has a son on the other team."

Michael's parents did not grow up here, so Mrs. Greenblat doesn't have any reason to recognize Bill. This is both relieving and irritating.

"Does he remind you of anyone?" I ask.

"Not really. Why, who do you think he looks like?"

It's ridiculous to think she would say me, but my hopes droop a little, like old flowers. "No one."

Forget Michael, all I can see now is Maybe-Bill. He is sitting with two other men, laughing and eating, and yelling at the umpire like everyone else. Except everyone else has a reason to be here — what's his? Denise said my dad moved out West right after high school, and that was the last anyone heard of him, so why is he back now? And why is he at a local minor baseball game?

Part of me wonders if this has something to do with the wedding. Mom said it was no big deal, but maybe she had tracked him down to let him know about it. What if I had come up?

Benji and I sometimes play the what-if game: "What if you won a million dollars?" "What if you lived forever?" "What if you could time travel?"

This game of what-ifs is not as much fun:

What if Mom called Bill because Doug wanted to adopt me?

What if Bill said no?

What if Bill decided he wanted me to live with him?

The what-ifs are so consuming, I don't even notice when Mrs. Greenblat takes Theo from me.

***

Finally, the game ends. I have no idea who won.

"Here he comes, our star player!"

Our star player? Sometimes I wonder what Michael tells his mom about me. Does she think we're dating, or just friends? It's something I would like to know the answer to myself.

Michael jogs over to say hi to his brothers and accepts a kiss on his cheek from his mom.

"Off to the Dairy Bar, I suppose," she says.

After every game, the team goes to the Dairy Bar for ice cream. Sometimes I come along, although Michael's teammates never know how to act with me around. Sometimes it's like I'm not there at all, and other times they act so stupid I *wish* I wasn't there.

"Have fun and remember not to eat too much. A full stomach before bed always gives you nightmares."

Michael blushes but doesn't say anything.

"And make sure you walk Clarissa home."

I've been scanning the crowds for Bill, and now I spot him, heading for the school parking lot.

"Actually, I can't come tonight."

Michael shrugs. "Okay. See you later?"

"Later," I agree. "Bye, Mrs. Greenblat!"

I rush away, trying not to look too eager and hoping they don't notice that I'm heading toward the parking lot, which is in the opposite direction from my house. I force myself to walk, but what I really want to do is run. The man who might be my dad is not that far ahead of me. He has sort of a bouncy walk. It makes him seem friendly. I watch as he takes his keys from his pocket and presses a button. The lights on a little black car flicker as the doors unlock automatically. I start to jog a little, not caring how I look. I'm not sure what I'll do when I catch up to him — I don't want to talk to him, but I'm not ready to let him disappear out of my life.

"Hey, Bill! Wait up!"

My breath catches in my throat as someone behind me calls out and Bill turns around. It has to be him. What are the chances that a man who looks just like my father would just happen to have the same name? I sidestep toward a tree at the edge of the parking lot and linger there. The man jogs past me and catches up with Bill, and the two stop to talk next to the car. As they do, I take the time to study everything about him and the car.

Now I know two things for sure: My dad is back in town, and I have his licence plate number.

Planning Day

After Bill's car pulls away, I run all the way home. I don't think I've ever run so far before, but I'm so full of adrenalin I do it easily. As I charge up the steps, I hear Mom and Doug doing dishes, and my heart constricts. Partially because of all the running, but also because I don't know what I'll say to Mom when she asks how the game was. Instead of facing her, I yell, "I'm going to Benji's!" through the screen door and run next door before either of them can say anything.

I ring the doorbell, but no one answers. In the semi-darkness, I grope around under the doormat for the key to Benji's house. I find it and jam it into the lock, my fingers shaking. All my stomping and fumbling must have drawn Benji's attention, because he is waiting for me when I stumble in. He looks stricken and is gripping the phone in one hand. "What's wrong?" he asks.

"Didn't you hear the doorbell? I rang it like six times!" I don't mean to sound so angry, but I'm so mixed up it just comes out that way.

"I was on the phone," Benji says.

"At this hour? With who?"

"Clarissa, are you okay? It looks like you're having trouble breathing."

After a few ragged breaths, I'm able to say, "I think I saw my dad."

"Who?" Benji asks.

I don't blame him. I can hardly believe it myself. "My dad. Bill Davies, father at large?"

Benji looks woozy. "I think I need to sit down."

"*You* need to sit down? What about me?"

I follow Benji to the living room. He sits on the couch, and I collapse on the floor, leaning my back against the cool leather of the couch, trying to steady my breathing.

"Tell me from the beginning," Benji says.

So I tell him about finding the yearbooks and the Google search and seeing Bill at the baseball game. When I'm finished, Benji says, "And you're sure it's him?"

"It looked just like him."

"But those yearbook pictures were old."

"He looks exactly the same. Older, obviously, but the same."

Benji pauses. "So you saw pictures of him, and then you saw a man who looked like him."

"It isn't someone who looks like him, it IS him. That guy called him Bill."

"Bill's a pretty common name."

"It was him, Benji! Why won't you believe me?"

"The whole thing is kind of unbelievable."

I sigh. "I know."

"What are you going to do?"

"I have to see him again."

"Are you going to talk to him?"

"I don't know yet. What would I say? 'Hi, Dad?'" I laugh even though it isn't funny. "I think I need to see him and then maybe I'll know what to do."

"Are you going to tell your mom?"

"Do you think I'm stupid? Of course not! She'd probably mess everything up."

Part of me wonders if she already knows he's here, which means she deliberately didn't tell me.

"So what's next?"

"That's why I'm here. I need your help. I got his licence plate number at the ball game."

"What good is that?"

"It was the only thing I could think of at the time."

* * *

Brainstorming calls for snacks. You can't think well on an empty stomach. The Dentonator doesn't like to cook, so Benji's house is always full of delicious, ready-to-eat things — unlike my house, which is stocked with carrot sticks and flax crackers and things that need peeling. First, Benji finds us some root beer and a super-size bag of ketchup chips to fuel our brainstorming session. Next, he appoints himself secretary and begins taking notes. After a few minutes I ask him to read me the list from the top.

"Things we know," says Benji, pausing dramatically. "Suspect looks like Bill Davies; suspect responds to the name Bill; suspect's licence plate number is BKJR 199; suspect drives a black car."

"Stop calling him 'suspect.' He isn't a criminal."

"Sorry." Benji sucks his can of root beer dry, then chews on the end of his straw. "If he was a criminal we could get the police to run his licence plate number and they could track him down."

"You watch too much TV. Anyway, if we walked into the police station looking for a car, they'd call our parents in about ten seconds."

Benji pales a little, probably at the thought of telling the Dentonator that the police want to talk to him. "Okay, so no police."

"No anybody," I say sternly. "Promise me Benji: this is just between us."

Benji nods. "I promise."

We munch in silence for a little bit. Even though we don't really have a place to begin, my spirits have lightened. It feels good to be planning this together, like one of our missions. Maybe all the missions we'd been planning and executing the past few years were leading up to this — the mission of all missions.

"So are you going to bike around town, looking for the car?" Benji asks.

When he says it out loud it sounds crazy, but that's exactly what I was thinking of doing.

"That's a lot of cars," he continues. Then his eyes light up. "Unless . . ."

"Unless what?"

"What if we look up all the Davieses in town and bike by those houses? There can't be that many."

"Of course! He's probably staying with relatives. Who else do you stay with when you come home? Benji, you're a genius!"

Benji looks pleased with himself.

"But if Bill has relatives here, that means I have relatives here . . ." I trail off, unable to say what I'm thinking. If my father has relatives here, why haven't they tried to contact me?

"Maybe we should stop by the hotel, too," Benji says.

"And the bed and breakfast," I add, happy for a change in subject.

Benji flips the notebook to a fresh page. "New list!" he announces. "Places to stay in town."

"And just outside, too. Like the Lilac Motel," I say.

Benji shudders. "That place is creepy," he says. "There are never any cars in the parking lot."

"Perfect! We'll be able to spot his car right away!"

Benji's eyes widen. "You mean we're really going to bike out there? In the dark?"

"Not tonight, Benji! Jeez!"

"Thank goodness. Because there are horror movies that start that way."

"You really do watch too much TV. Make sure it's on the list," I insist.

Dutifully, Benji adds Lilac Motel in his meticulous writing, doodling a thunder cloud and lightning bolt around it. I watch him add a drawing of a car on the bottom of the page. It's very good, even though Benji doesn't salivate over cars like some boys do. I guess you don't have to like something to be able to draw it well. He even writes Bill's licence plate number in the right place.

"How's the wedding planning coming?" he asks.

"Fine. Mom still doesn't want to make a big deal out of it. It's just a casual thing, in our backyard."

"Who's coming?"

"Not a lot of people. Mom said I could invite you, of course, and Mattie. And maybe Michael."

"Is he your date?"

"No, just a guest."

"Aren't you supposed to bring a date to a wedding?"

"It's not *that* kind of wedding. Why, who would you bring? Charity?"

"I was just asking." Benji blushes, and I wonder if maybe

she is the nighttime caller he has been spending all his evenings chatting with. I used to think Benji was maybe just a little in love with Charity, but he swore up and down it wasn't true: they were just friends and he admired her. I want to ask more about it, but Benji changes the subject on me. "How is living with Doug?"

"Weird."

"Weird how?"

"Just weird. Imagine if all of a sudden there was a woman in your house walking around in boxer shorts or singing songs you've never heard of in the shower."

"She probably wouldn't be wearing just boxer shorts," Benji says.

"You know what I mean."

"But you like Doug, right?"

I shrug. "Yeah, doesn't make it any less weird."

"Maybe it will always be a little bit weird," Benji muses.

I throw a pillow at him. "Way to cheer me up."

Benji laughs as the pillow skims the top of his head. "You could do a lot worse than Doug," he points out.

"True. Your dad could've moved in," I tease.

"Hey!"

And with that, I've started a full-out pillow fight.

Mission Day

Dear Clarissa,

I just read your letter and OH MY GOSH! I can't believe you saw your dad! It has to be him, don't you think? It's too much of a coincidence that we were looking him up online and all of a sudden a man named Bill, who looks exactly like him, just happens to walk into your life! The world works in mysterious ways. You HAVE to keep me updated. Write me every day if you can! Otherwise, I won't be able to sleep — I'll be too full of curiosity!

Every day, Wicker writes a new saying on the chore board outside our cabin. We're supposed to think about it all day, and then we talk about what it means and how we can incorporate the meanings into our daily life. I've been keeping track of them in my journal. Here are some of my favourites:

Don't count the days; make the day count.

Only boring people are bored.

Shoot for the moon, and you'll land among the stars.

Aren't they inspiring? Just reading them makes me feel braver. Hopefully they do the same for you. Here's another one just for you: change only happens to those who are ready for it. Isn't that a good one? Try to keep it in mind! Maybe even write it down somewhere, so you can read it when you need strength.

I haven't had a letter from Benji yet. He's probably busy with the showcase. Are we still going to see it together? If you want to go with Michael, I understand, but is it okay if I come, too? It's okay if you'd rather go just the two of you. I don't want to be a third wheel.

Miss you (but only on days that end in y),

XOXOXO

Mattie

P.S. You haven't told me if you and Michael are official yet! Don't think I've forgotten!

***

I wait for Benji outside the theatre, wondering if it is, in fact, possible to sweat to death. I have to remove my backpack, which is hot and getting heavy. Inside are some snacks, my mother's grade twelve yearbook and our list of places to investigate.

I'm sitting beside my bike in the only shady spot, flipping through the yearbook while I wait. I stop again on the autograph page, trying to figure out the inside jokes behind the weird messages.

Dear Annie, if modelling doesn't work out, maybe you can be a personal assistant? The next time someone gives me a sunlight surprise, I will say no. Seriously though, you rock! Marilyn

Yo, Beauty Queen! How come you never went out with me? I'm better than a hundred Jacks! Thanks for making English worthwhile! The Greg-meister!

Jack? Who is Jack? Didn't Greg mean Bill? Is Jack some sort of retro slang for boy?

I flip to the class photos to look for this mysterious Jack, but then Benji arrives with his bike. I snap the book shut and spring to my feet. "Finally!"

"I said three o'clock; it's only three-ten."

"What were you doing?"

"I had to say goodbye to Charity and everyone. Plus, Dean was giving me advice about my song."

I should probably know who Dean is, but I've been so distracted with the wedding and my dad showing up that I can't quite remember. "Who's Dean again?"

Benji looks at me like I'm crazy. "The director? He's a university student? He does, like, *real* plays in the city. He's running camp this summer."

"Right. Here, I brought food." I reach into my backpack and fish out a sandwich that is now more of a squished ball of bread and peanut butter. I hand it to Benji. I guess the food got a bit beat up with the yearbook and the water bottles clanging around in there. "Can you eat and bike at the same time?"

Benji looks insulted. "Of course."

"Then let's go. First stop, Mason Street."

It turns out there are four Davies families in town with listed phone numbers. The closest is on Mason Street.

It's so humid it feels like we're pedalling through soup, the thick, split pea kind. Even the breeze we generate by biking feels hot; though it does lift the lank and heavy hair off the back of my neck, cooling it from forty degrees to thirty-nine.

I can't wait to get my licence. Considering the helmet, backpack, pedalling and the lack of air conditioning, biking has to be the hottest form of transportation.

Mason Street is deserted: no kids playing street hockey or elderly people hanging out on porches. This makes spying easier. The plan is to bike by 184 Mason Street, laughing and talking, while scanning cars in the area for the licence plate number, which we have both memorized. If we see the car, we have to say, "Cramp!" at the top of our lungs. It's the perfect code word. Anyone around will think we just need a breather, not that we are staking out a house.

"What if we have a real cramp?" Benji asks.

"Then say 'Can we stop? I have a cramp,' or anything else! Just don't yell out 'Cramp' as one word!"

"I was just asking. Calm down!"

"I can't calm down! My *father* is in town!"

Turns out the code word was even more appropriate than we thought. I have cramps all over my stomach. These ones are from anxiety, not biking. All I want is to find out where he's staying, so I can eventually do something about it. What if we ride by just as he's getting out of the car and he waves and says hi? Then what will I do?

It turns out I don't have to worry about it yet, because there are no cars in the driveway at 184 Mason Street. The cramps loosen a little.

"Maybe everyone's at work," Benji says.

"Why would Bill be at work if he's just visiting?"

Instead of answering, Benji asks, "What's the next address?"

If you don't count the Lilac Motel, 439 Birch Street is the furthest address on our list. That's where we head next.

I haven't been able to convince Benji to bike to the motel yet, so it's last on our list, followed by three question marks. We bike single file though town, taking the scenic route by the river because I thought it might be a bit cooler by the water, and because biking through major intersections makes Benji nervous. It adds five minutes to our travel time.

My stomach cramps up again as we slow to our leisurely pace on Birch Street. I spot a car, but it's red, and sure enough, the licence plate number is wrong, too.

"Two more, then we check out the hotels," Benji says.

Victoria Street and Grosvenor Park are also big fat failures. There are lots of cars at the Super Eight Motel, but after three rounds of the parking lot, none of them are right, either. By the time we get to the River's Edge Bed and Breakfast, I'm hot, irritated and in need of a win.

No such luck.

"The River's Edge is pretty fancy," Benji points out. "More for tourists. Bill isn't exactly a tourist."

He's right, but it doesn't make me feel better. I savagely kick at the kickstand and rear my bike around in the opposite direction. "Let's go home. I'm boiling."

Benji hurries to catch up. "Can we stop and get freezies?"

"I didn't bring any money."

"I have some."

I don't say anything, but I let Benji lead the way. He takes us to a 7-Eleven and gets two giant freezies: red for him, blue for me. I perk up a little. Blue has always been my favourite. I'm not sure what flavour it is — raspberry, blueberry, some kind of berry — but it doesn't matter, it's pure delicious. Benji forgot to ask the cashier to snip the top, so I have to tear it with my teeth. I open Benji's, too, since even his teeth are too delicate.

It feels good to tear into something ferociously when you're in a bad mood.

"Let's go to the river to eat them," Benji says.

Right now, with my skin so hot and sweaty it's prickling, the river sounds perfect. "Okay."

***

A few summers ago we discovered our own secret part of the river. Well, not secret — none of the river is private. But every time we came to cool off, we were the only ones there. Less than a ten-minute bike ride from our houses, it has a small strip of beach (gravel, mostly), a willow tree that neither of us is brave enough to climb and a boulder that juts out from the water, perfect for sunning yourself after you cool off in the water.

As hoped, there is no one else around when we arrive. So far this is the luckiest thing to happen to me all day. I let my bike fall, whip off my backpack and helmet and step out of my shoes, heading for the water. The river isn't deep, so the water isn't very cool. But after all that biking, it's still refreshing to feel it slosh against my ankles. I grab fistfuls of my shorts, yanking the hems up as high as they'll go, and wade out a bit further.

Benji takes his shirt and shorts off, folds them neatly and places them on top of his helmet. He wades in up to his waist, wearing just his boxer shorts, and then sinks into the water, carefully keeping his hair from getting wet. At the back of his head a cowlick stands straight up. He looks like a duckling.

"It's really nice!" Benji says, dogpaddling in circles around me.

"Don't rub it in," I say.

"It's not that nice," he says dutifully.

I wish I could take my clothes off as well. There was a time when I would have whipped off my shirt and shorts and dived in with only my underwear on, too. Benji is more like my brother than a friend. But back then I didn't wear a bra. Everything changes when you start wearing a bra.

I scratch furiously at the clasp, as if it's the source of all my problems.

"I want to go in, just for a minute. Can you turn around?"

"Sure. I'm going to dry off, anyway." Benji hauls himself onto the sunning rock. Not only does he face the other way, but he closes his eyes and covers them with his hands. As quickly as I can, I wiggle out of my shorts and sweaty t-shirt, tossing them at the edge of the water. Then I wade back in, plug my nose and plunge into the river. It feels wonderful.

Underwater, I turn my head slowly, loving the feeling of my hair floating around me. When my nose starts to burn, I emerge, shaking the water from my ears.

Benji is still sitting with his back to me, eyes covered. I slip my t-shirt back on and haul myself onto the rock beside him. I leave my shorts on the bank. My shirt is long enough, plus it will dry in about five minutes. Wet shorts take forever to dry out.

I'm surprised to find that there's barely enough room for the two of us on the sunning rock. The last time we were here, we comfortably sat side by side. Benji scooches over without ever opening his eyes.

"You can look now."

Benji takes away his hands and blinks at me in the sunlight. "Better?"

"Better. I feel like I can think now. "

"So what do we do next?" I like how Benji says "we." It makes me feel less alone.

It's strange, but tracking down my father has made me feel lonely. Shouldn't I feel like I've found something?

"Maybe he went somewhere on a day trip," I suggest.

"Or he's visiting someone."

"Or he just happened to be out driving when we went by."

There are lots of perfectly good reasons why Bill's black car was not in any of the driveways we saw, but this doesn't make me feel any better. It makes me feel stupid and at a loss for what to do next. Being a detective is hard. Especially on a bike.

"Maybe we should try again, early in the morning before people go out for the day," I say.

"But still late enough that the sun is up, right?" Benji really hates the dark.

"We still haven't checked out the Lilac Motel," I point out.

Benji has a handful of pebbles that he is tossing one by one at the water, attempting (but failing) to make them skip across the top. "I know."

"I can go by myself, if you're that scared."

"I'm not scared; I just think it's far. We'd have to bike on the highway."

I resist rolling my eyes. Benji can be such a scaredy-cat sometimes.

"Really, you don't have to come if you don't want to. I can make it there in less than half an hour, especially without you slowing me down."

"Don't go by yourself," Benji pleads, and he looks so pitiful I have to relent.

"I won't," I say, but I don't mean it.

"We should probably go back now."

Benji and I bike all the way home without a word. We're both too busy thinking. But before he goes inside, Benji turns to me and says, "That was nice, today. It felt like one of our old missions. Remember those?"

I smile for the first time that day. "Yeah, I remember."

I'm glad I'm not the only one.

Rainy Day

It's been raining for days. As happy as I am to not be melting into a puddle of human stink, I'm ready for the sun again.

Business has slowed at the Hair Emporium, and I spend most of my days doing crosswords and stuffing wedding favours into gauzy gift bags.

Originally the plan was to make donations to the Breast Cancer Society in each guest's name, but Mom decided that they needed to have a take-away, too. So she is giving everyone a little sample bottle of her favourite moisturizer and a scented candle, along with a hand-lettered card that reads *A Donation Was Made to the Breast Cancer Society on Your Behalf*. My job is supposed to be writing the cards, but my handwriting is functional at best. Fancy lettering is really more of a Benji task, but he's not around to do it, which leaves me.

Needless to say, it's a dull way to spend a day, so when the bell jingles at the top of the stairs, I practically leap out of my seat to greet the person who will save me from dying of boredom.

"Is that Clarissa Louise Delaney or a starlet I see down there?"

At first I don't recognize the woman making her way down the stairs, shaking the rain from her jacket and smoothing her long, dark hair. I can tell by the way it's puffing out that she has been flat-ironing her natural wave into submission. Someone needs to tell her you can't win when rain is involved. Then I get a better look at her, and despite the rain my whole day brightens.

"Tina!"

Tina Cooper is probably the coolest of my mom's friends. "Hey, girl! You're looking better than ever." She raises her hand for a high-five. She is the only adult I know who can get away with this without looking hopelessly lame. She is also the only white person I know who can call people "girl." Unfortunately, she moved away years ago and only drops by a few times a year when she's in town visiting family.

"The boys must fall all over themselves when they're around you. Have you got a boyfriend yet?"

Before I can say anything, Mom emerges from the storeroom, her arms full of shampoo bottles. "Tina?" The bottles almost hit the floor, but Mom recovers, dumping them in the nearest styling chair, and rushes over to give Tina a hug.

"Did I know you were coming?" she asks.

Tina shakes her head. "Nope. I'm in town visiting my sister and thought I'd pop by and see if you could fit in a trim."

Mom gestures to a styling chair. "At your service!"

"The word is you're getting married, Annie."

Mom shows off her ring. "Guilty as charged."

Tina claps and bounces a little before wrapping my mom in yet another hug. Maybe constant hugging is something that friends do when they get older. Although when I try to picture Benji and me falling all over each other, it doesn't stick. Mattie, of course, is already an experienced hugger.

"Congratulations! I want to hear everything!" Tina shrugs off her purse and blazer and sinks into a recliner.

Normally I'd find myself a magazine to read, but it occurs to me that since Tina knew Mom in high school, she must have also known Bill. I need to find a way to bring him up in the conversation.

"Clarissa, can you get Tina a drink?"

Shoot! The one time I want to stick around and eavesdrop and my mother is sending me out of the room.

"You don't want to miss out on Clarissa's iced lemon-tea," Mom says. "She makes it herself. Her secret ingredient is mint."

"How can I say no to that?" Tina says with a wink.

I run up the stairs two at a time, while Mom fluffs out Tina's hair to assess the job ahead of her. I'm in such a rush to get back downstairs that I miss the glass while I'm pouring. Lemon-tea sloshes down the side and onto the counter. I don't have time for this! I can't miss any of their conversation. What if they're going to reminisce about the Good Old Days? I need to be there for every little detail.

I am careful on the way back down, having already lost time wiping up my first spill.

"Here you are; I hope you like it. I can add more lemonade or mint if you want," I say, putting on my most professional and helpful daughter face.

Tina takes a delicate sip. "This is delicious!" she says, smiling at me. "Clarissa, you're a girl of many talents!"

"Thanks," I say, as I sit down and get comfortable.

"Now, Annie, tell me about this man of yours."

"What do you want to know?" Mom says demurely. "His name is Doug Armstrong, and he owns a fitness centre here in town. We met almost a year ago, when I started training at the gym. Then we started dating a few months back, and things just went from there."

"Look at you — you're positively glowing!" Tina says. Then to me, "Isn't your mother beautiful?"

"She is," I say. "The most beautiful woman in town."

Mom raises her eyebrows at me, and I decide to tone down the perfect daughter routine. I may be laying it on a bit thick.

Tina leans in, all conspiratorial. "What do you think of Doug, Clarissa? Is he good enough for our girl?"

"He's great! Really friendly. And tall. And nice to dogs . . ." I am struggling with things to come up with, but Tina seems to think this is enough.

"Dog lovers are good people," she says. "When's the wedding?"

"Two weeks, if you can believe it. We're just having a small party in the backyard with a few friends."

"Sounds perfect," Tina says.

"So what's new with you? How's work?"

Tina starts talking about her son and her job as a speech therapist, and I zone out for a little bit, trying to come up with things to say to direct the conversation toward high school.

I have a pen and paper ready, so when they start talking, I can jot down names and anything else worth investigating later. As it turns out, I don't have to say anything, because eventually Tina launches into it all on her own.

"Have you seen any of the old gang lately? TJ? Alison? Stookey?"

Mom shakes her head. "Not really. I lost touch with a lot of people once Bill and I called things off. Stookey wouldn't look me in the eye, and Tyler Kellerman never spoke to me again."

I can't believe my luck. Mom never talks about Bill so candidly. At least not in front of me. My heart is beating so hard, I can feel it throbbing in my fingers. I can barely hold the pen as I write down *Stookey* and *Tyler Kellerman*.

"Those guys were always tight," Tina says. "And you know what Alison was like: if Stookey said jump, she said how high."

"I know. They got married soon after high school. They're divorced now."

"What about Tara B. or Krista Cummings?" Tina asks.

"No one's really seen or heard from Krista since she went off to university, and Tara moved to Toronto a few years ago. Last I heard she was working in TV doing publicity or something."

"Good for her."

"Do you ever hear from Matt?" Mom asks.

Tina groans a little, embarrassed, then looks at me and explains, "Matt Van de Graff was my first boyfriend. I can't believe you're bringing him up, Annie!" She swats my mother playfully and continues, "I thought we were going to get married for sure."

"I always thought he was a sweetheart, even if he did try too hard. You were a cute couple."

"He *was* a sweetheart and probably still is."

"He's working for his father now. He'll take over Van de Graff Farms, if his father ever retires. He married Janet Simmons. They have three kids."

"Good for him. Matt is a great guy. Remember how he hero-worshipped Bill?"

Mom nods. "I remember. It's too bad. How come nice guys always look up to jerks?"

"Because girls like a bad boy," Tina says. "Then we grow up and kick ourselves for ever thinking like that. But Doug sounds like one of the good ones."

"He is," Mom says.

"How's Denise?" Tina asks. "We've been trying to get together, but our schedules never match up. God, I miss that laugh."

I have to restrain myself from choking. Denise's laugh, as distinctive as it is, is not something one should pine over.

Once the conversation veers into a discussion about Denise and makeup products, I sense that my fact-finding mission has come to an end. I look at my list: Stookey, TJ, Tyler Kellerman, Alison, Krista, Tara B. and, perhaps most promising of all, Matt Van de Graff. Surely some of these people are still in touch with Bill. And at least one of them, Matt Van de Graff, still lives in town. Now all I need is a plan.

Wednesday with Denise

I have a one-track mind. Bill is all I can think about. Even though "Mission: BKJR 199" went bust, and I still haven't decided what to do with my list of names, I'm not ready to give up. I need to gather more information, which is why I volunteer to pick up the punch bowl and plastic champagne glasses from Denise's apartment.

Mom gives me a quick squeeze before I go. "Thank you for being so helpful. This party is really coming together, thanks to you."

I roll my eyes. "Party? Don't you mean wedding?"

"You know what I mean. I'm really impressed with how calmly you're taking all of this. I know it's a lot to digest. You would tell me if you needed to talk, right?"

Truth be told, the wedding is only the second most important thing on my mind these days. Maybe I should be thinking more about Doug becoming a part of our lives forever, but finding Bill feels more urgent. Who knows how long he's in town for? The window of opportunity is small, and it feels like it's shrinking every second I'm not out there doing something about it. He could have left already.

The thought makes the back of my throat tickle, like I'm about to cough — or worse, cry.

"I'd tell you," I say, and in my head I add silently, *just not about what I'm really doing.*

"What did I ever do to deserve such a great kid?"

I smile weakly and am out the door before the guilt makes me confess. If only she knew I was about to secretly pump her best friend, she of the famously loose lips, for information on my long-lost father.

I've only been to Denise's apartment a handful of times. Her building is one of four by the river. All of the apartments on the north side of the building overlook the water. It's a nice view — just ask the people who used to have it. When the apartment buildings went up, they were wedged between the backyards on Dawson Street and the strip of woods that backed up to the river. The people who lived in the houses complained, but they couldn't do anything about it.

It was in the paper a lot. Denise used to read the stories aloud to Mom and me in the Hair Emporium. "Boo hoo," she said, rolling her eyes. "Poor little rich people have to share their view with us regular people. Cry me a river."

You have to buzz to get in, and then take the elevator up. Denise lives on the fourth floor. I'm so full of anxious energy, I could probably run up all four flights and keep on going to the tenth floor, but time is ticking, and I don't want to waste a second.

"Welcome, welcome!"

Denise's house is a mess. No matter where you look, it appears as though she were interrupted in the middle of something and forgot to go back and finish. The table is full of breakfast bowls with cereal bits dried to the bottom and dinner dishes with crusts of hardened spaghetti sauce. A coat, two pairs of shoes and a blouse lie on the back of the couch, as if she changed clothes on her way out the door. Romance novels lie open — pages down, spines cracked, making little tents — on the couch, the kitchen counter and the floor in the bathroom.

I am something of a neat freak and the whole messy place sets my teeth on edge.

"Don't mind the mess. When you live on your own, no one sees it, so what's the point?"

"Personal hygiene?"

"Oh, you're such a funny girl. Want a root beer?"

"Yes, please." Denise disappears into the fridge, which is just as jam-packed as the rest of her apartment. When I catch sight of a watermelon balancing on an egg container, I have to avert my eyes. I can't help counting the disasters waiting to happen.

"How's the wedding planning going?" she asks.

"Fine, although Mom still refuses to acknowledge that it's a wedding. She keeps calling it 'the party.'"

Denise shakes her head. "Has she changed her mind about music at least?"

"No! I suggested a whole bunch of nice, non-wedding songs, and she still thinks it would be too formal."

We don't agree on much, but music at my mom's wedding (or non-wedding) is one thing Denise and I are both pushing for.

"Well, we can keep at her, but if Annie doesn't want to do it, she won't." Denise gives me a very pointed look. "Must be a family trait."

I ignore the last bit and take the root beer she offers me.

"Do you think she'll change her name?" I ask.

"I doubt it," Denise says.

"Annie Armstrong sounds too much like a country singer. Delaney is a good last name," I say carefully, looking for a way to ask what I really want to know. "I like being Clarissa Delaney. I'm glad she never went with Davies. Clarissa Davies sounds like a high school secretary."

"With press-on nails," Denise snorts. "But Davies was never in the cards for you, kiddo."

"Why not?"

Denise narrows her eyes at me. "Why do I feel like this is a trap?"

I play innocent. "What do you mean?"

"I mean, why are you bringing up your father's last name?"

I look down at my drink and fiddle with the pop tab. "Mom and I found her old yearbooks. It just made me think."

"Don't you have enough to think about right now? Why bother wasting your time and energy worrying about him?"

"Was I always going to be Clarissa Louise Delaney? Did she even think of Davies?"

"You're her child; why shouldn't you take her name?"

"And my grandparents, I mean, on his side, they were okay with it?" I can't bring myself to use his name, Bill. I'm afraid that if I do, something in my voice will give the truth away. She'll guess that I've seen him and have been out looking for him.

"Haven't we had this conversation before?" Denise asks, trying to change the subject.

"Not exactly."

"Yes, I do believe we had this exact conversation at your house, sitting at the kitchen table, not so long ago."

"Well, now I have more questions."

"Lord, give me strength." Denise downs her root beer in one long gulp and rubs her forehead.

I decide to come clean. Well, partially clean. "I saw a picture of my dad."

"Who?"

Honestly. Between Denise and Benji, you would think that I popped out of the world completely fatherless: a miracle of immaculate conception.

"What do you mean, who? Bill Davies, obviously."

"Why would you go looking for him?" Denise says with a sigh.

My heart stops. How does she know? Then I realize she means looking for him in the yearbook, not looking for him in town. I have to swallow hard to keep my voice casual.

"I wasn't looking for him; he was just there, in the year-book."

"I don't believe that for a second, but okay, if you say so."

"In the yearbook he seemed . . . fun."

"Oh, he was fun all right," Denise says, but she doesn't elaborate.

"There was this picture, I think it was from prom. They were both all dressed up, but he was joking around for the camera, in sunglasses."

Denise nods. "I remember that picture," she says.

"How come he never came back here? Doesn't he have family?"

"His parents were divorced and he lived with his dad. As far as I know, Mr. Davies moved away years ago. He had an older brother, but I don't know what happened to him. I doubt he has much of a reason to come back."

Except for me, I think. Aren't I enough of a reason?

"In the yearbook it seemed like they were really in love."

"They were young and beautiful, of course they were in love. It doesn't mean it was going to last. You can't believe everything you see in a yearbook. Those things are meant to make high school look perfect, when lots of the time it was far from it."

"Do you have yours?"

"No, I got rid of them ages ago."

"How come?"

"They made me sad."

"They're just some cheesy old books; how can they make you sad?"

"This might be hard for you to believe, knowing me as I am now: great skin, great hair, all put together—"

Bite your tongue, Clarissa, I think. This is not the time for a snarky comment, even if there are a hundred things to say.

Denise continues, "But when I was in high school, I was a bit of a dork."

I think of her school pictures, the big smile and big hair, but I stay silent.

"Thank goodness for your mother; otherwise, no one would have looked twice at me. But I always thought, just wait, I'm going to move to L.A. and make everyone jealous."

Denise gets up and starts to pace, like she did in those first few weeks after she gave up smoking. At her side, her fingers drum against her thigh: yet another one of her smoking withdrawal signs.

"Back then, I used to think I would be a makeup artist on movie sets — the kind of person who could charge a thousand bucks for a few hours on Oscar night, glamming up celebrities. And what do I do now? The same thing I've done for almost fifteen years: I sell makeup in hick towns to people who think blue eye shadow is still the height of fashion."

"But you have a job, and this apartment . . ." I'm about to add "and your health," but it feels like something a guidance counsellor would say.

"My job is a joke, and I don't own this dump; I rent it," Denise says savagely. She stops pacing and makes a bee-line for a cupboard, fumbles around and pulls a package of cigarettes out from behind the coffee mugs. Uh-oh, this isn't good. Denise stopped smoking more than a year ago when my mother was in treatment. Now she only smokes when she's stressed out. I just wanted some answers; I didn't mean to drive her to smoking again.

"Don't tell your mother," she says, indicating the cigarette.

"I won't, as long as you don't tell her about this conversation."

Denise blows a stream of blue-grey smoke out both nostrils. "Wouldn't dream of it. Look, I don't want you to think I'm some sad, old single lady. I've got plenty of good years in me yet, and I'm going to make some changes. Oprah always says you have to be the change, not just wait for it." Denise exhales, closing her eyes. "But you can see how I wouldn't want a bunch of old yearbooks around, mocking me. Making me feel like the same old geek I was back then."

I don't know what to say. I'm uncomfortable giving advice to my own friends, let alone adults. I drink my root beer and wait for the mood to change. How did this mission get so completely off track?

"Just a second — don't go anywhere."

Denise disappears, leaving me on the couch, sipping

my root beer and trying not to touch the piles of clothes on either side of me. Who knows how long they've been there or whether or not they've been recently laundered? She returns with an album, baby pink and laminated, with enormous pastel circles and squiggles on the front. It is the ugliest photo album I have ever seen.

"This is all I have left from high school. Sort of like my own yearbook, except I got to choose all the pictures."

Denise lets me flip through the pages, which are stiff and covered in slightly greasy laminate. Most of them are shots of Denise and an impossibly young-looking version of my mother, modelling hairstyles and playing for the camera.

"Your mom used to let me practise on her," Denise says. "When I got really good, I did her makeup for all the beauty pageants."

Some of the photos are group shots, taken in the hallways of the school or around someone's truck at a party in the country. I ask Denise for everyone's names, as if it makes a difference, knowing who the people are.

"Who's that?"

"That was . . . Lord, I don't remember his name. It'll come to me."

"It wasn't that long ago."

"I know. I just haven't thought about him in ages."

"But you look like you're such good friends in this picture. Or at least he and Mom do."

"Well, sure! At the moment we probably felt like the best of friends. But people change, life moves on and then, the next thing you know, your friend's kid is accusing you of being a bad person because you can't remember the name of some guy you went to a party with once."

I ignore that last part and press on. "I bet Mom would

remember. Look at her — it's like they're best friends!"

Denise shakes her head. "She might have really liked him, but I doubt it. Your mom knew how to work it. She was a big flirt; she made everyone think she loved them. Part and parcel of being a Dairy Queen, you know."

I'm not sure I like the idea of my mom being a flirt, even if it was part of her beauty queen persona.

I continue to flip through the album while Denise half-heartedly cleans up around me, occasionally peeking over my shoulder to comment on so-and-so's dress or sigh about how skinny she used to be.

And then I come to a photo of my parents. It was taken on the steps of the school. Mom is sitting a few stairs below Bill, leaning her cheek into his knee. He has his hand in her hair, mussing it up a bit, but from the way she's smiling, she doesn't seem to mind. Bill looks right at the camera and smiles, no mugging, no jokes, just pure happiness. Even though it's a nice picture, it makes my heart ache. Why do some people stay in love and others fall out of it? Most kids have tons of pictures of their parents — on their wedding day, or on vacation, or cuddling them as babies — but other than that grainy yearbook photo, this might be the only picture in the whole wide world of my parents together and happy.

"Take it," Denise says.

I have to swallow the lump in my throat before answering. "Are you sure?"

"Why not? He's your dad, even if he is a lost cause." Denise looks at me sternly. "And believe me, he is a lost cause. Don't waste your time and energy on him, Clarissa. It's not worth it."

I hope my cheeks aren't as red as they feel.

"It is a nice picture, though. One of my best."

"Thanks."

I peel back the laminate and gently work the photo off the page. The back is gummy from years of being sandwiched between the sticky photo page and the cracked plastic, but otherwise it's in good shape.

"You're welcome. Keep it in a safe place, and don't tell your mother I gave it to you."

"I won't."

"Good. It'll be our secret."

Denise and I have a lot of little secrets, things we tell each other that we can't share with my mother. We smile at each other, co-conspirators.

"Now what was I supposed to give you again?" she asks.

"The punch bowl and leftover plastic champagne glasses."

"Ah, yes."

Denise retrieves the punch bowl from the top of the fridge. It's so dusty, it looks like it has a fine layer of fur. I wait a few more minutes for her to rinse it out, trying not to gag when she pulls the dishcloth away all slimy and disgusting.

"There you go, glasses and a bowl for the world's most understated wedding," Denise says.

"It's not a wedding; it's a party," I say, doing a dead-on impression of my mother.

Denise throws her head back and hoots with laughter. It's good to see her back to her loud, honking self. I'm in no hurry to see the frantic, smoking Denise again anytime soon.

"That's perfect!" she cries. "You are something else. Have a good night, kiddo, I'll see you soon. And don't go worrying about sad, old Denise. The world hasn't beaten me yet. You caught me at a bad moment. I've got something up my sleeve."

That night I do something I thought only people in movies did; I put the photo of my parents under my pillow. I'm not a complete idiot, I put it in an old plastic frame from the dollar store first. But it's the only place I know my mother will never look. Also, a very tiny part of me, probably the same part of me that used to believe in the tooth fairy, hopes that somehow sleeping with it so close by will bring me luck.

Phone Day

Dear Clarissa,

You're a genius! I am picturing you sitting in the Hair Emporium, pen in hand, taking notes like a real detective! This might be your most exciting scoop yet. Have you tracked down the people on your list yet? Do any live in town? I was thinking that you could call them and pretend to be part of a committee, trying to get more information about people for a reunion. You always said you wanted to be an actress, so here's your chance to practise your acting skills!

I wish I was there with you, although today we went kayaking and Wicker said I was advanced enough to have my own kayak! Isn't that great? It's much easier than I thought it would be. If you ever come to camp, I can show you how. Or you can be my buddy and we can share a double kayak. I wouldn't mind sharing, as long as it's with you.

Can you believe the summer is almost over?! I'll be home in less than a week, and the next thing you know WE WILL BE IN HIGH SCHOOL! I know it's too much to hope we'll be in all the same classes, but at the very least maybe we'll be in the same homeroom. Sir John A. isn't that big, but it's still way bigger than

Ferndale. Promise me we'll sit together at lunch!
  Miss you (but only on days that end in y),
  XOXOXO
  Mattie

Mattie's letter is exactly the kind of motivation I need. First, I bring out the yearbooks. It turns out that TJ and Tyler are the same person — Tyler (James) Kellerman— and Stookey is probably James Stookey's nickname. Both of them were in the same grade as my parents. I cross Alison, Krista and Tara B. off my list, since it didn't sound like they were in town. Plus, it seems more likely that Bill would have kept in touch with the guys in his circle, not the girls.

"Clarissa?"

I snap the yearbook shut, even though Mom is calling to me from down the hall and she can't possibly see through my door. "Yes?"

"I'm going to the gym, and then Doug and I will pick up some groceries on the way back. Do you need anything?"

"I'm fine!"

"I'll be back in less than two hours. Don't forget to let the dog out."

"I won't!"

Perfect. With Mom and Doug out of the house, I can make my phone calls without either of them walking in on a conversation. That would not be a phone call I'd be eager to explain.

I wait for the sound of the car starting before really getting ready.

Suzy sits in my doorway with a stuffing-less toy monkey in her mouth, ready to play.

"Look, Suzy, I'm sorry that you want to play and everyone left, but I can't deal with you right now." I feel bad, but I shut the door in her face.

I don't know why I bother talking to her. It's not like she understands me.

I decide my name will be Sarah, and that I am a summer student gathering information for a reunion. I jot down a few questions to ask, just to make my cover story sound legitimate.

After pacing in my room and doing a few jumping jacks to get rid of my nervous energy, I'm ready. I tell myself this is just like a play; I am preparing just like Benji or Charity would before a show. First up, Tyler "TJ" Kellerman. As luck would have it, there is only one *Kellerman, T.* in town. The phone rings and rings, making me more anxious each time. Finally, just when I think the voicemail will pick up, a woman answers.

"Hello?"

"Can I speak to a Tyler Kellerman?"

"Who's this?"

"I'm calling from the Sir John A. Macdonald reunion committee and I was wondering—"

"Sorry, we're not interested."

"But—"

Too late. The surly woman hung up on me.

I guess I didn't think this through. I'm going to have to find a way to immediately let people know I'm not looking for money, or else they are all likely to hang up on me. And now I've wasted a perfectly good opportunity. I can't call back and pretend to be a different person looking for Tyler, or that woman will get suspicious. I cross Tyler Kellerman off my list.

In the hallway, Suzy starts barking.

"Shush, Suzy!" I say sharply. I can't have her making

noise in the background. What kind of office has a dog? She's totally going to blow my cover.

I decide to try Matt Van de Graff next. The Van de Graffs have two meat markets, one in town and the other in Hickson. This makes them pretty easy to track down, as long as you stick to the business numbers. There are about a million Van de Graffs listed in the residential numbers, so I start with the market in town.

"Van de Graff Meats, how can I help you?"

"Hi, is Matt Van de Graff working today?"

"No, sorry. Can I take a message?"

"No, thanks, I'll call back."

Shoot. I have no luck with the first five Van de Graff residential numbers listed. But by now I'm not even a little bit nervous. I guess all it takes is a few phone calls and you get used to it.

"Hello, could I speak with Matt Van de Graff, please?"

"Speaking."

"Hello, Mr. Van de Graff, my name is Sarah, and I am a summer student on the Sir John A. Macdonald reunion committee. Can I talk to you for a few minutes? It won't take very long, and I'm not asking for money."

Matt laughs. "I can tell by your spiel people have been hanging up on you before you can get to the point."

"Yes," I admit.

"Well, I've got a minute or two. Go ahead."

"Great! First, would you be interested in attending a high school reunion?"

"Well, sure. It would be nice to catch up with some of the old gang."

"Would you rather attend a reunion in the fall, spring or summer?"

"Summer is probably best."

"Do you know a William Davies?"

"Bill? Of course, I do. I've known him for years."

Finally, a lead! I will myself to stay calm and ask, "Do you have his current address and contact number? It's not in the system. I only ask because I'd love to invite him as well."

"I know it's here somewhere, but my wife keeps all that information in a little address book. I can't say where it is exactly, but I'm sure I could track it down and call you back."

"So would you say you're in regular contact with Mr. Davies?"

"I wouldn't say regular, no."

"And he lives with his family . . . ?"

"It's probably best you get all the nitty-gritty details from him. I can't say that I know what his current situation is, for sure."

I can tell I won't get anywhere else with Matt Van de Graff. I need to end the conversation before it gets suspicious. "Well, thank you for your time, Mr. Van de Graff. I will update our files, and someone will be in touch with you if we get enough interest in a reunion."

"No problem. I think it's a great idea. If you still need Bill Davies's info, give me a call back in a few days, and I'll have it for you."

"Thanks, Mr. Van de Graff. Have a great day!"

I hang up feeling strangely elated, even though I didn't get any useful information. Just talking to someone who knows Bill now, in the present, makes him even more real to me.

Next is James Stookey.

"Hello, can I speak with a Mr. James Stookey?" I am really getting into the swing of things as Sarah, summer student extraordinaire. I pretend to be as perky as Mattie and as polite as Benji, but with my own Clarissa flair.

"That's me."

"Hello, Mr. Stookey. My name is Sarah, and I'm a summer student working on the Sir John A. Macdonald reunion committee. Can I talk to you for a few minutes? It's only a few questions, and I'm not calling to collect donations."

"I guess so. What do you want to know?"

I go through my dummy questions, establishing myself as a legitimate committee member, before launching into the good stuff.

"Thank you for your answers, Mr. Stookey—"

"You can call me Stookey; Mr. Stookey is my father." Stookey laughs, so "Sarah" laughs along with him.

"Okay, um, Stookey. I'm having a bit of trouble tracking down a classmate of yours by the name of William Davies. Do you know him?"

"Billy boy! Of course I do! What do you need to know?"

"I don't seem to have updated contact information. Do you know how I can reach him?"

"Sure I do. I'm happy to give you his number, but it won't do you any good calling him up in B.C."

"Why not?"

"Well, as luck would have it, he's in town! I had dinner with him just the other day."

Even though I already suspected this, having seen him with my own two eyes, the confirmation still makes my fingers tingle. "What a coincidence."

"He doesn't get back here much, but he turned up a few weeks ago, looking to see his kid."

If my heart was an elevator, it would have dropped twenty storeys, all the way to the bottom of my toes. After a moment, I manage to say, "His what?"

"Yeah, he's been out of the picture for a while, but he figured he'd show up and put in some face-time. I think he's at the Lilac Motel if you want to try him there."

I don't hear anything else Stookey has to say; I couldn't possibly hear anything over the sound of the blood pounding in my head. I know he's still talking, because there is a buzzing in my ears, but I forget all about polite Sarah, the summer student, and hang up the phone. I'm feeling excited and sick and completely out of sorts. Not only is my dad in town, but he's here to see me.

Bad Day

"Pick up, pick up, pick up," I mutter, but to no avail. The phone keeps ringing on Benji's end. He's not there. As usual. For a moment I consider calling Mattie at camp. Surely they let campers take emergency phone calls. I imagine a counsellor taking her out of dinner and walking her up to the office for her phone call. Knowing Mattie, she'd probably imagine the worst: car accident, fire, kidnapping. But once I got the chance to explain everything to her, I know she'd see my side. I need her right now. Especially with Benji distracted and on a no-phone diet.

I'm so desperate to talk to someone, I almost call Michael. But I'm not sure he'd be very good in this situation. I feel like I'm still just getting to know him. What I do know is that he's only just started looking at me when I talk to him, and I don't want to jinx anything. Not that there is anything to jinx.

Why is no one around when I have important things to discuss?

I hear the car pull in, then Mom and Doug laughing as they make their way up the front steps and into the kitchen. The laughter stops abruptly, and I hear my name being called — and not in a happy dinner's-here-come-and-get-it kind of way.

"Clarissa, get out here."

I shake out my excitement, put on the most normal face possible and meet Mom and Doug in the kitchen. They're standing at the counter, both looking grim for people who are getting married in a few days.

"What's up?" I ask.

"You tell us," Mom says, meaning her-and-Doug us, not me-and-her us, like it used to be.

"Um, nothing?" I say, trying to remember if I've missed something. Neither of them appear to have changed their hair or bought new clothes since they left.

"What have you been up to?" she asks.

"Nothing," I say quickly, wondering if it's possible that she called to check up on me and I missed the call-waiting beep.

"This whole time?" she presses.

"Pretty much."

"Follow me."

I don't want to follow her anywhere, given the chilly tone of her voice, but I don't have much choice. I follow her into the living room where she stops in front of a damp spot on the carpet. Not far away, Suzy is huddled by the screen door, whining.

Uh-oh.

"Did you let the dog out like I asked you?"

"No," I admit. "But she didn't whine or bark or anything."

"According to you."

"She didn't!" I protest. "I would have heard her!"

"And would you have let her out?"

"Yes!"

"Clarissa, you've made it very clear that you're not pleased about the dog, but this is not the way to retaliate."

"I'm not retaliating! I didn't hear her! I just forgot!"

Now Doug speaks up, "Exactly, you forgot. I need you to start remembering these things, Clarissa. You've got to step up and show some responsibility."

"Oh, so now I'm Clarissa? What happened to C-Bot? Or C-Money? I guess now that you got what you wanted, you don't need to try and win me over with those stupid nicknames."

"Clarissa," Mom's voice takes on a warning tone, but I can't stop now.

"I'm sorry that *your* dog can't control her bladder, but I don't see how that's *my* problem. Nobody asked me if I wanted a dog, and if they had, the answer would have been no. So explain to me why it's my job to walk her and look out for her and clean up her messes when she's the one in my house?"

"Our house," Doug says, maddeningly calm.

"No, *my* house. I've lived here my whole life; you've been here for ten minutes!"

"I'd appreciate it if you lowered your voice, Clarissa. I don't deserve to be yelled at like this."

The more Doug talks, the angrier I get.

"You don't get to tell me what to do. Just because you've moved in doesn't mean you get to call the shots. You're just my mother's fiancé, someone I have to put up with. You're not my father!"

I watch Doug's face to see if the insult lands the way I intended it to, sharp and stinging like a slap. But instead of wounded, he looks steely and impenetrable.

"Are you going to your room?" he asks calmly.

"Yes, I think I will."

Doug nods. "I think that's a good idea. I also think you

should stay in there for a while until you cool down and are ready to apologize."

Now I'm the one who feels slapped. I look at Mom, who makes no move to defend me or step in. When it becomes clear that they've both finished with me, I storm back to my room and stay there all night. Not because Doug told me to, but because I want to.

Dinner comes and goes, and even though I can smell the hamburgers sizzling, I don't budge. I'm too angry to be hungry, and I can't stand the thought of their self-righteous faces sitting round the dinner table looking all smug and superior. Now that he's fully entrenched in our lives, Doug has shown his true colours. Turns out he's not the carefree, happy-go-lucky dude he makes himself out to be. He's just another stuffy adult with stupid rules, who's never in the wrong. Well, I don't care how well he thinks he can play the role of my father. Neither he nor my mom can tell me what to do.

Tomorrow, I find my dad.

Shopping Day

I go against all of my natural instincts and wake up at seven o'clock. That way I can catch Benji before he goes to rehearsal and tell him the plan.

Now more than ever, I have to get to the Lilac Motel. Before it was a risk, but now that I know Bill is in town looking for me, what have I got to lose? The sooner I track him down, the better.

I'm waiting for Benji on his front stoop when he comes out, ready for drama camp. He is so surprised, he almost drops his backpack.

"What are you doing here?"

"Today is your half day, right?"

"Right."

"Perfect! Today is Lilac Motel day. I know he's there now; his friend Stookey said so. We'll go right after rehearsal, so it will be daylight and no one can kidnap us."

Benji frowns. "You shouldn't joke about stuff like that."

"I'm kidding! It won't take that long; we'll be back before dinner."

"I can't."

"Benji, it's totally safe!"

"It's not that. I want to go with you—"

I give him a look, and he changes his tune.

"Well, I don't love the idea, but I still would go with you. Except, I'm busy."

"With what?"

"Stuff for the play."

"Of course!"

"Don't be angry; Dean needs me!"

"I need you more! Benji, I found something out yesterday. Something about my dad. I think he's here, looking for me! Don't you see? I need to get to that motel."

"Then why doesn't he come to your house? It's not a secret that your mom lives here."

"Oh right, and have Mom beat him to death with a curling iron? Think about it, Benji! He can't show his face here. I have to get to him before he gives up and leaves."

Benji doesn't respond. Not even a sad smile or a shoulder shrug.

"Fine. I'll go by myself."

Benji looks truly alarmed. "No! Don't! Can't you wait until tomorrow?"

"It can't wait another day! He could be gone by then. Maybe he's left already."

"I'm sorry, but I can't today. I already promised Dean."

The expression on Benji's face is so miserable, it's hard to stay mad at him. It doesn't mean I'm not upset, though, because I am. I feel ditched. All I say is "Fine."

"Promise me you'll wait?"

"You know me better than to ask me something like that," I say. I turn and stomp away.

Maybe I should have been more understanding, but the truth is I'm annoyed. I know the showcase is important to Benji, but there will be other plays. Possibly meeting my dad is a once-in-a-lifetime chance.

I have tried to be patient and understanding with Benji where theatre is concerned, even though it's hard because I was the one who was interested in acting in the first place. Is it so much to ask that he give up a few hours to come with me while I track down my dad for the first time ever? There is definitely something up with him. The old Benji would know how important this was to me. This new Benji, with his fancy showcases, new hair and plaid shirts, sucks.

I hear our screen door creak as I walk back home, and Mom appears, tea in hand, stooping for the newspaper. I'm relieved it isn't Doug. I'm still mad at him. I'm still mad at Mom, too. I'm not ready to forgive her for not sticking up for me last night. She is as cheery as ever and remarks, "You're up early!" as if nothing happened.

I'm too angry to respond, so I continue to glower silently after Benji, even though he's long gone. Mom, the eternal morning person, is undeterred. "What are you up to today?"

"That is yet to be determined," I say, still fuming.

"Then I'll determine it for you. We're going shopping for dresses after lunch."

I won't have time to bike out to the motel and back before then, especially if I want to factor in any time for father-daughter bonding.

"But—"

"No buts. And Denise is coming with us. She may not be a bridesmaid in the traditional sense, but she's getting a new dress all the same."

Shopping is one of my least favourite activities, next to going to the dentist and algebra. But I'd rather spend a whole day in the dentist chair, finding the value of X, than spend one hour shopping with Denise. I prefer Denise in small doses and I'm still recovering from our confusing heart-to-

103

heart the other night. Why is the whole world conspiring to keep me from meeting my father today?

***

Dress shopping is overwhelming. Mom refuses to go any-where with the word "bridal" in its title, so we end up wan-dering into every store in the mall that carries dresses of any kind. There's so much to choose from, even though we've limited ourselves to the bargain racks. The depart-ment stores are the worst. Just when you think you've seen everything, there's a whole other section

As usual, Denise is full of advice: "If I had that waist, you can bet I'd be showing it off," and "I know people keep saying coral is flattering, but if I were you, I'd stick with something less orange."

Eventually a tired-looking saleslady comes over to ask if she can help us find anything.

"We need three dresses," Mom says.

"Three?" I repeat.

"Yes, three," says Mom. "You, me and Denise."

"Me? Why me? Can't I just wear something in my closet? I thought this was all about you and your special day," I protest, but Mom doesn't budge.

"Lucky for you, I'm willing to share my special day."

The saleslady perks up considerably. "You're getting mar-ried?" she asks.

"Sort of," Mom says.

Denise snorts. "Sort of? Annie, I know you're trying to keep this small and everything, but it doesn't mean you have to tiptoe around the issue. You're getting MARRIED for crying out loud! If it was me, you can bet everyone from here to Buckingham Palace would know!"

Mom relents. "Yes, I'm getting married. But I want it to be a casual affair, nothing fancy, no bows or bustles or tulle. Just a nice summer dress, appropriate for an afternoon party."

The saleslady searches aggressively through the racks, throwing dresses over her arm. She holds them up one at a time for Mom to okay or veto, then sends us into the fitting rooms with the winning options. For some reason, Denise feels the need to give the whole fitting room a play-by-play of her experience.

"Bless that woman. She brought me a size eight. I haven't been a size eight in years. How's it going in there, Annie? Which one are you trying on first?"

"The strappy little sundress. Are you ready?"

"Ready."

"Clarissa?"

At my mother's insistence, we all have to come out wearing the first option at the same time.

"Clarissa? You all set?"

There is no use ignoring them. "Ready," I grumble.

I unlatch the lock of the stall and step out between Mom and Denise in a dress that is too strapless, too pink and absolutely not right for me. To my left, Denise has squeezed most of herself into a turquoise tube dress. It is too tight over her hips, and the zipper looks like it gave up halfway up her back.

"All that running and I still can't get into an eight," she mutters. Then to me, "You look cute as a button; what are you frowning about?"

"It's too pink," I say.

"Look at your mother over there. Just stunning! You've still got it, Annie."

It's true. My mother is wearing a white sundress that not only fits perfectly, but shows off her midsummer tan. If possible, it even makes her hair look blonder. The saleslady returns and stops in her tracks to gasp over the sight of my mother.

"Simple and gorgeous," she says. "If you ask me, you can call off the search now."

She doesn't mention Denise or me.

Mom shrugs. "I like it, but I want to try the others before making a decision."

We disappear back into our stalls for round two. My second dress isn't much better, but at least it isn't pink. The sleeves are made of lace and it has a ribbon threaded around the middle that can be cinched into a bow. It looks like something a flower girl would wear, and I am much too old to be a flower girl.

"Do you want Clarissa and me to match?" Denise calls over the walls of the stall.

"Doesn't matter," Mom says. "If you end up picking two dresses that match, so be it. I just want you to feel beautiful. Ready for round two?"

"Ready as I'll ever be."

"One, two, three."

We emerge again, my mom in a long, flowing dress that looks more beachy than bridal to me. Denise is in a black, strapless dress. Mom gushes over Denise's outfit.

"You look gorgeous, DeeDee! So sophisticated."

Denise does a number of turns, checking herself out in the mirror. "I do, don't I?" she muses. "Are you sure you don't mind me wearing black at your wedding?"

"Not at all. Now, Clarissa, you look adorable."

"Exactly. Seven-year-olds look adorable. It's too young."

To my surprise, Denise agrees with me. "You're right. No more lace or ribbons for you. What would Michael think, eh?" She winks at me, and I march back into my stall for option number three. Even inside my stall, I'm not safe from interrogation.

"Is Michael coming?" Denise asks.

"I'm not sure yet," I reply. The truth is I haven't asked him.

"That boy is a cutie. Has he kissed you yet?"

That I don't answer.

My mother laughs. "Now, DeeDee," she says, but she doesn't exactly tell her to lay off.

Then suddenly Denise bursts into loud, honking tears. I unlatch the door and step out to see what happened. As far as I can tell, she isn't injured, and there isn't anyone else around who could have done anything. There's a click, and Mom rushes from her own stall to Denise's side, still in option number two. Seeing Denise cry isn't all that unusual; she cries all the time. She cries during *The Bachelorette*, for goodness sakes. I just don't understand why she's crying now. I try to remember if I said something to upset her, but unless she has something against Michael, I don't know what I possibly could have done. Maybe she's still feeling unhinged from the other night.

"I'm going to miss this," she says, then collapses into my mother's arms. Denise is not a pretty crier. Unfortunately, we have that in common. When my mother cries, delicate tears well up in her big blue eyes, and her face turns slightly pink, like a Disney princess. Denise and I are slobbery, red-faced snotty messes, but this doesn't bother Mom. She lets Denise slobber all over her shoulder, while she rubs circles on Denise's back and makes cooing noises.

"I know, DeeDee. Me, too. Me, too."

It's an odd sight: six-foot-tall Denise crumpled on the shoulder of my five-foot-three mother. I stare at them, two grown women hugging it out in the women's fitting rooms at the Bay, and I wonder what they're not telling me.

"What's going on? What are you going to miss?"

Denise sniffs and runs her fingers under her eyes, trying to mop up the mess of mascara and eyeliner that is travelling down her cheeks.

"Denise got a big promotion," Mom says. "She's moving to Mississauga in the fall."

My mouth drops open so quickly, I can actually feel the joint pop. I probably look like one of those cartoon characters — bug eyes and my jaw dragging on the ground. It takes real effort to close it.

"You never told me," I say, thinking of all the quality time I spent with her the other day, and she didn't mention a single word about a promotion.

"I just accepted the job this morning," Denise says. "I've been thinking about it for a while, and now seems like the right time."

"What will you be doing?"

Denise tries to laugh, but all that emerges is a shaky, uncertain noise, like a choked cough. "They want me to train salespeople. Can you believe that?"

Actually, I can. "You convinced Dolly to wear lipstick after sixty years of her wearing no makeup at all. Think of what you can teach people who already love lipstick." This is probably the nicest thing I've ever said to Denise. I am rewarded by a fresh bout of wailing and having my face crushed against her chest in a wet hug.

Mom puts one hand on Denise's shoulder and strokes her

hair with the other. "DeeDee, you've earned this! Think of the opportunity."

Denise relaxes her grip to wipe her eyes again, and I seize the opportunity to wriggle from her grasp. She fishes a Kleenex out of her purse, blows her nose with an enormous honk and says, "You're right. I know you're right. I've lived here my whole life, and what do I have to show for it? A crappy job, a crappy apartment and no love life." Denise sighs. "Maybe there's someone waiting for me in Mississauga."

Mom smiles. "I know there is."

Denise manages to get a grip, and the search for my dress is back on. I trail behind Mom and Denise as they sift through discount racks of sundresses. I don't want to intrude on their time together, especially since it has an expiry date now. I've never noticed it before, but they talk in half-sentences, almost like their own language.

"What about—"

"Yes, but the thing—"

"You're right, it's too—"

"—fussy."

"Not like that other one."

"With the neckline?"

"Exactly."

The saleslady is smart enough to leave us alone. I can see her watching us from a few racks over, but she has clearly been scared off by Denise's theatrics. We find a few more options and head back to the change rooms try them on.

My favourite is a white dress with tiny straps that comes just to my knee. I've never worn anything so girly before, but unlike that piece of pink frosting I had on earlier, this one looks nice. I know I've made the right choice when I see

Mom's face light up as I come out of the stall.

"Well, look at you," she says. "My young woman." Then she is overcome by an embarrassing rush of mothering and kisses my cheek repeatedly. I resist the urge to wipe it off. I admit, I like what I see in the mirror. The dress is white and floaty, but in a summery way, not a princessy way.

Denise is getting teary-eyed again. "You're just so big," she says. "When did you get so *big*?" I frown. Would it be so hard to say tall? What's with all the "big" talk?

Mom twists my hair and holds it at the top of my head. "We'll do an up-do and get you some nice earrings; you'll be a stunner."

Stunner. I've never been called that before. I like the way the word tickles the hairs at the back of my neck.

"Wait here." Mom ducks back into the stall and emerges a moment later in her first dress, which looks very similar to mine: white, knee-length, spaghetti straps. The only major difference is Mom's is fitted and classic, like something from a black-and-white movie, and mine is only fitted at the top, the skirt loose and breezy. We stand side by side, looking at each other in the mirror. The similar dresses emphasize our differences. Short, tall. Blond, brunette. Straight, curly.

I wonder what she sees when she looks at me. Is she reminded of my father? Does she ever wish I looked more like her? Does she ever think about him? I want so badly to ask, but now is not the time.

I wonder if there will ever be a time.

The saleslady comes in and claps her hands in approval. "How lovely. I know of a couple of wedding parties where the bride and her daughter dressed alike. It makes for a nice picture."

"You don't think they look too similar?" I ask.

"I think they're perfect," Mom says.

After we pay for our dresses, Mom turns to Denise and says, "Now, shoes!"

"Shoes?" I'm not up for another half-hour of trying things on and spontaneous weeping. "Can I go to the food court?" I ask.

Denise frowns. "You just had a snack. You want to be able to fit into that dress, don't you?"

Normally I'd make a joke. I've always considered making fun of Denise to be my job. But the thought of not having her around to laugh at is so startling, I can't think of a single thing to say. I feel completely thrown, like someone just told me that drinking water is actually bad for you, or England is a made-up place that never existed. Typical Denise: just when we start to get along, she decides to move hours away.

"I think Clarissa has reached her limit," Mom says. She hands me a five-dollar bill. "Go ahead. Meet us out front in forty-five minutes."

I hurry away before she can change her mind.

Mall Day

The mall is full of back-to-school shoppers and people looking to escape the heat. I wander in and out of stores aim-
lessly, enjoying an ice-cold Frappuccino (what my mother
doesn't know won't hurt her) and not shopping. The back-
to-school displays make my stomach turn.

Usually Mom and I do a one-stop, back-to-school shop
(binders, shoes, maybe a pair of jeans). Then we have an
end-of-summer barbeque with Benji and Denise, followed
by my annual back-to-school haircut. School is less than two
weeks away, and Mom hasn't mentioned any of it. I wonder
if she's forgotten in all of the wedding/Denise-moving-away
madness. Or maybe, because I'm going into high school,
she thinks I'll be too old. I hope not; I like the tradition.
Besides, I don't feel any older than I did last year.

I veer toward the food court, staying away from anything
that looks like it could be used in a classroom. Fries will
take my mind off school. Maybe even poutine.

I'm in line, trying to decide if I should get a small or a
medium, when I spot Benji sitting with a boy I don't know. He
looks older; maybe he's a senior. He's handsome, in a boy-band
kind of way, and he's deeply tanned, with unnaturally sculpted
hair. The vee of his t-shirt is a little lower than necessary.

When Benji spots me he looks surprised, then guilty, then waves me over. "Clarissa! Hi."

"Hi. Who's this?"

"This is Dean. He's directing the show."

So this is the famous Dean. Funny, they don't appear to be doing show stuff that was so important, Benji absolutely could not miss it.

"Clarissa! It's so nice to meet you!" Dean stands and gives me a big hug. Even after hanging out with Charity and some of Benji's other theatre friends, I still can't get used to how touchy they are. "Benji is always telling me hilarious things about you."

"Oh, really?" I shoot Benji a look, wondering what exactly he's telling this stranger that is so hilarious.

"Not 'ha-ha' funny," Benji says, but he doesn't elaborate.

"So what brings you to the mall?" Dean asks.

"Shopping," I say flatly, not ready to share my business with this freakishly pretty stranger.

Benji laughs, but it sounds forced. "See? Hilarious!" he says weakly.

"What are you doing here? Shouldn't you be at the theatre?" I ask.

"No, rehearsal ended a few hours ago, but I had some show-related errands to do, costumes and stuff, and I know that costumes are Ben's forte, so I brought him along. Now we're just hanging out, having some ice cream. Want a bite?" Dean offers me a spoonful of vanilla ice cream that is dripping something that looks like melted plastic, but is probably strawberry sauce. I shake my head no.

"Costume design is one of *Ben's* many fortes."

Benji blushes, but Dean doesn't seem to notice. Instead he laughs and says to Benji, "You're right, *so* hilarious!"

"I can't believe you went shopping without me," Benji says.

"I could say the same about you. How do you think I feel, dragged to the mall against my will, only to find my best friend — who was too busy this morning to help me — having a great time in the food court?"

Benji starts to explain, but I don't want to hear it.

"It wasn't my idea, obviously. As you know, I had other plans today, but my mom made me. Denise came, too—" I am about to say something funny about her struggling with the zipper, but then I remember that she's moving, and the words get stuck in my throat. Again.

Benji looks at me expectantly, waiting for the punchline, but there isn't one that doesn't make my throat ache.

"Who's Denise?" Dean asks.

"She's Clarissa's mom's best friend," Benji explains, then he actually rolls his eyes, something he almost never does. "She's crazy. Fun, but totally nutso."

I am shocked at how casually the insult rolls off Benji's tongue. Making fun of Denise is my job; *he's* the one who always defends her. Dean nods like he knows; it makes my skin itch with irritation. He doesn't know anything about me or Denise. How dare he nod his head! And how dare Benji pretend that he doesn't come running over when he hears Denise cackling away at the TV!

"She's more than that! She's like my aunt. And she's moving."

I practically spit the words out. Benji turns two shades paler in shock. I'm a little shocked myself. I've never called Denise my aunt before, although that's basically what she is. Denise has been at every birthday party I've ever had, whether I wanted her there or not. She calls to wish us

Merry Christmas on Christmas Day, and she's the one who stayed with me when my mom was in the hospital. Maybe she's not related to me by blood, but isn't that what aunts do?

"She's moving?" Benji repeats. He looks as stricken as I feel.

"That sucks," Dean says.

"Yeah, it *sucks*," I say, thinking this glossy idiot couldn't possibly know the depths of how much this sucks. I can feel tears starting at the back of my eyes. I can't believe I'm about to cry over Denise. In the *mall*. I have to get out of here.

"Well, I should go. They're probably looking for me."

Dean stands up and looks at me with concern. "Hey, are you okay?" When he touches my elbow I actually flinch. What is with him? A normal person would see that I was upset and leave me in peace.

"I'm fine, but I really should go. Bye, *Ben*."

***

I'm so angry when I get home that I have to do something or I'll explode. There are still a few good hours before sundown — I can make it to and from the Lilac Motel if I hurry. I tell Mom I'm having dinner at Benji's and grab two granola bars to eat on the way. I pack my helmet, the yearbook and bicycle light, and away I go, taking matters into my own hands.

Later that Day

As I pedal to the Lilac Motel, I think of all the rumours I've heard about it. Like the one about the old man who died of a heart attack. No one found him for three days, and only then because he had started to rot and the smell caught the attention of someone's dog.

Then there's the story about an old medium who lived there years ago. People came to visit her, looking to talk to their dead relatives. She's no longer there, but the ghosts of the people she contacted still haunt the Lilac's rooms.

I've even heard that the restaurant turns into a seedy club at night. But I'm sure none of it is true. People love stupid stories. Though it is true that the Lilac Motel has been closed down and reopened at least three times, and there must have been some reason for that each time. Maybe there is a tiny kernel of truth in the stories.

I'm feeling chilled, despite the heat and the warm wind I'm creating as I bike along the shoulder of the highway. Think about Bill, I tell myself. Think about your father who came thousands of kilometres across the country to see you.

I don't see many cars, which is fine by me. Normally biking near cars doesn't make me nervous, but the cars in town go much slower than the cars on the highway. My bike wobbles a little in the draft they create as they sail by at eighty, ninety, even one hundred kilometres an hour.

One more hill and the Lilac Motel is in sight. Just in time, too. My calves feel tight, and my mouth is completely parched. There are three cars and a van in the parking lot. One of the cars is black. It looks like the car I saw at the school parking lot, but until I see the licence plate, I can't be sure.

I'm still on my bike, my left foot off the pedal and resting on the ground. I'm waiting for the traffic to pass so I can rush across the highway. I grit my teeth to keep from screaming in impatience. Where are all these cars coming from? Thirty minutes of almost no traffic, and all of a sudden there's a mini-rush exactly when I want to cross.

Finally the rush is over, and I pedal like mad across the street and into the parking lot. I cruise by all the empty spots, nearing the little black car, saying the licence plate number over and over again in my head: BKJR 199. BKJR 199. BKJR 199. When I get to the black car, I stop, just to be sure.

BKJR 199. This is it — Bill's car.

Now what? The parking lot is deserted. Everyone is either in their rooms or in the restaurant. The Lilac Motel is divided into two wings that reach out from the restaurant and lobby in the middle. I guess that's where people go to check in. Each wing has five purple doors, each with a small window, which I assume means there are five rental units per wing, ten in total.

I could wait out here for him to come out to the car, but I don't want to get caught loitering around the parking lot. People could get suspicious and call the police, mistaking me for a car thief. I could go in and ask for him at the desk.

Maybe they could call him for me. But then I would have to know exactly what I want to say.

I take a deep breath, sucking in thick, soggy air. So much for deep, cleansing breaths.

It's dim inside, the lobby lit with a ragtag collection of lamps in corners and on the front desk. A man with a walrus mustache and a belly that is barely contained by a sickly orange shirt is slumped in a chair behind the front desk.

"Excuse me, I was wondering if you could call Bill Davies for me?"

"Did you try his room?" the Walrus asks.

"Actually, I forgot his room number, which is why I was wondering if maybe you could call him?"

The man harrumphs into his mustache and reaches for the phone. Even this small movement is almost too much for the buttons of his shirt, which are threatening to pop right off. I take a step back and to the side, out of range.

Every part of me feels like it's on high alert, like one of those wind-up toys full of gears and things that whir and spin. My nerves are jangly and my knees feel like jelly. It's impossible to get myself together. I tell myself to keep breathing as the Walrus waits for Bill to pick up on the other end. When he hangs up without saying a word, I deflate a little, like a day-old balloon.

"Not in," the Walrus says.

"But I saw his car in the parking lot," I say.

"Must be in the bar then." The Walrus gestures with his head to an even darker room just behind him. The only thing that separates it from the lobby is a podium with a *Please wait to be seated* sign stuck on the front. Beyond the podium, I can see tables, a bar and two TVs mounted in the corners of the room. It's dingy, but it doesn't look that bad, which is a relief. There are a few people seated at the bar, but I can't tell if one of them is Bill.

"You going in?"

It's now or never.

"Yes," I say.

I wait at the podium as the sign instructs, but after a minute it becomes clear that, in fact, no one is coming to seat me. So I shuffle in, hoping I don't look as lost as I feel.

Technically I am in a restaurant, not a bar, but I still feel like I am in some place that I shouldn't be. Even the smell of french fries can't hide the underlying musty stench of the place, which smells like an old couch someone has left outside in the rain. An older man and woman are sitting at a table staring up at one of the wall-mounted TVs. They don't talk; they just sit and watch the baseball game, occasionally picking at the food in front of them. A pair of men are chatting with the bartender; both are wearing baseball caps and holding tall glasses of beer. A fifth person sits alone at another table, fiddling with his phone, an untouched beer and an open newspaper in front of him. Bill.

I make my way to his table, willing him to look up and see me, but he is wrapped up in whatever he's doing on his phone. If he would just look up, surely he would see a resemblance between us and instantly know that I was his long-lost daughter, come to find him.

"Mr. Davies? Mr. Bill Davies?"

Finally he looks at me. We make eye contact, and I almost lose my nerve. Then he smiles at me, and I start to thaw out.

"That's me. You look a bit young to be a waitress," he says, but I can tell by his tone that he knows I'm not the waitress, he's just teasing me. Charming, I think. Denise said he was charming. I try not to fall under the spell of his smile, which is as warm as the midday sun, and probably just as bad for me. My tongue feels heavy, and my throat feels gummy. I can't seem to get any part of my mouth to work. This is going to be even harder than I thought.

"I'm not the waitress," I manage to say.

"Okay, then. This is a strange place for a young lady," Bill continues, not unkindly. "Are you lost?"

"No," I manage to say.

"Well, then what can I do for you?"

"I don't know where to start."

He smiles again and says, "I always find the beginning is a good place."

I sort of thought by now he would recognize me, or at least see some of himself in me. "I'm Clarissa," I say. Then I puff myself up with a big breath and go on, "Clarissa Louise Delaney."

I wait for recognition to flash across his face, change his features, indicate in some way that my name conjures up something other than the blank smile that he keeps giving me.

"Delaney?" I repeat. "As in, daughter of Annie Delaney? As in, your daughter?"

After all this time, after all my agonizing over the perfect wording, that is not what I wanted to say. It was too dramatic, too sassy. I feel like a bad actress in a soap opera. But now that it's out there, I can't take it back. Bill laughs, takes his hat off and smooths his unruly hair back. I want to tell him not to bother; we have the same bouncy hair and nothing will hold that curl back for long. But I can't, because I'm confused by his laughing. It doesn't seem to be out of joy or relief.

"All right, you got me. Who put you up to this? Was it

Stookey? Tyler?" Bill looks around as if expecting ghosts from his past to jump out and yell *gotcha!* But it's just me, stupid me, and I wonder if I've made a huge mistake.

"No one put me up to it. It's me, Clarissa. Your daughter."

Bill squints at me, like he needs glasses. "Don't tell me it was Annie, not after all this time. She made it clear she was done with me when she ditched me for Jack Handover."

Jack Handover?

The Jack from the yearbooks?

"I don't know any of those people," I say, trying to think over the sound of my brain screaming WHO'S JACK HANDOVER? "I'm Annie's daughter. I'm your daughter."

"Okay, look, haven't you heard of taking a joke too far? You couldn't possibly be my kid. Annie would have told me — I would have known!" Bill says, charming smile completely gone. It makes him look older, more haggard than handsome.

Even though I knew that Mom had never told him about me, a little part of me thought that maybe he had known all along, deep inside — that maybe the feeling had grown so big, that he'd done a little research and found out about me and came to town to find me. That part is thoroughly and utterly squashed now. All I can say is, "You really didn't know?"

"You're not kidding?"

"No!"

Bill swears under his breath, though not so quietly that I can't hear him. "Jesus, Annie!"

"I'm Clarissa," I whisper, feeling the last of whatever pride I had shrivel up and die.

Bill gets up abruptly, bumping the chair behind him. It totters but doesn't fall. He rubs at his cheeks, as if they have answers.

"Of course you are. I just mean — Jesus, Annie! She

121

could've told me! Called, or even sent a goddamn email after all these years!"

"Then why are you here? Who did you come out to see?" I ask.

"My nephew's in a baseball tournament. He asked me to come see him play, so I decided to make a trip out of it. I don't get out here very often."

You can't hear a heart break, but you can certainly feel it. I know this, because I feel mine shatter into a million pieces that lodge themselves all over my body. In my fingers, in my toes, especially in my cheeks, which are burning red and smarting with embarrassment. All this time, that little part of me thought that maybe he was back because of me, but he was back for someone else. It wasn't me he was looking to get some face-time with, it was his nephew. I had the whole situation wrong.

"Does your mother know you're here?" Bill asks.

I shake my head no.

"Look, you shouldn't be here. Let's go call your mother, and we can all sit down and talk about this."

My vision blurs as the tears I've been trying to hold back take over. Bill sees this and touches my elbow gently, as if he's never comforted a kid before and is afraid I'll bite him.

"Please don't cry. I'm sorry I got all crazy. This is news to me, too, okay? But we'll work this out. What did you say your name was again?"

I can't help it, I am crying. I back out of the dark, dingy bar and run to my bike. I don't know if Bill is behind me, because all I can hear is my heartbeat. It feels like it's taken up residence right between my ears. I jam my helmet on my head, kick at the kickstand and book it out of there as fast as I can, far away from Bill and the Lilac Motel.

Even Later
that Day

I can't go home, and I can't go to Benji's. He is too busy with his new hair and Dean and the stupid showcase. But I do need somewhere I can go and be alone.

So I bike all the way to Michael's house, let myself into the backyard and head for his brothers' tree house. I climb up, not caring as the branches etch my skin and pull sharply at my hair. It's like I can't feel pain anymore. When I finally pull myself inside, I lie face down, spread-eagle, and pray for the horrible spinning sensation to stop.

What's wrong with my mother? She's the one who fell for him and got pregnant. How could she be so stupid? Didn't she know a snake when she saw one? Is that why she didn't tell him about me? And who's Jack Handover?

The last question makes me feel queasy. What did Bill mean when he said that my mom ditched him for Jack Handover? I've never even heard of him before. Then I remember I still have the yearbook in my backpack. Part of me wants destroy it — throw it into the river, or rip it apart page by page and feed each one to the barbeque — but first I need to find out.

It's dark, but I know David and Solly keep flashlights in the tree house — they showed me on one of my non-dates with Michael. There isn't a lot of room for storage up here, just a shelf with all the tree house necessities: flashlight, binoculars, comic books, balloons for making water bombs. I find a flashlight and flip through the incriminating yearbook, my nervous stomach turning somersaults in my belly.

I find him quickly. In his school photo, Jack Handover looks like a jock with a serious streak. His hair is perhaps a bit too gelled and stiff, but it looks like a respectable haircut, not wild and rebellious like Bill's bad-boy mop. His face is square, and he is gazing into the camera with a determined look on his face, like he can see his future and is just about to grab it. Did that future include my mother?

I don't have to search too hard to find out more about him. Jack Handover is splashed all over the yearbook. He played senior football and was on the wrestling team, so I was right about him being a jock. He was also a member of student council and the debate team. There is a candid photo of him painting a mural that features the school mascot, a fierce-looking badger. There's another of him posing with a group by a pick up truck, which is all dolled up as a float for the Santa Claus parade.

Bill wasn't in any club pictures. Aside from the mandatory school photo, the cheeky prom photo and his dedication page, he was absent from the yearbook. I should know: I have been searching every page for him for weeks now. Unlike Jack, he wasn't much of a joiner.

My mother was a member of both the spirit committee and the prom committee — not very serious clubs, like debating, but they are something. Is that how she met Jack? The autographs are sadly lacking in information. No one mentions Jack at all, and the only message that could potentially be from him is a bit of a stretch: *Hey, Annie! You should come out for student council next year! You already have my vote! –J*

"J" could be anyone, and according to the club picture, there were tons of people on student council. Probably more than one of them had a name that started with the letter J. Or maybe "J" wasn't even part of student council, but just thought that my mother should be. I feel like I'm going crazy. I thought that talking to my dad would finally complete the picture, not bring up all these other questions.

I start to snuffle, and then snort, and then I'm crying. Soon I'm bawling like a baby in my maybe-boyfriend's little brothers' tree house. I'm pathetic, unwanted. No wonder Bill freaked out. What father would want me as a daughter?

Then I hear a screen door slam. My sobs dry up as I watch a beam of light bob cross the backyard toward the tree house.

"Hello? Is someone up there? I suggest you show yourself before I call the police," says Mr. Greenblat.

I stay absolutely still.

"I have no problems setting our guard dog loose," he adds.

Well, that's a joke. Rambo may be named after some terrifying killer from a movie, but unless being covered in wet puppy kisses is torture, I'm not in any real danger. Still, I am technically trespassing.

I drag myself to my knees and stick my head over the edge of the tree house. I blink down into the light from the flashlight, which is surprisingly strong.

"It's just me, Clarissa," I call down, knowing full well that the rest of the Greenblats (and probably the neighbours) are watching this spectacle from their windows.

"Oh, Clarissa," Mr. Greenblat is taken aback. The violent flashlight beam lowers in surprise; then he aims it directly at my eyes, but I'm too tired to shield them from the light. "You shouldn't be here so late."

He thinks I'm a bad influence. One of *those* girls. The kind that sneaks out in the middle of the night to prey on unsuspecting boys in a tree house. The kind that cheats on her boyfriend, or gets pregnant in high school. Like my mother.

"I know, I just needed to think," I say, feeling about a hundred years old. "Michael doesn't know I'm here. I came here on my own." At least he didn't know before. He probably does now.

"Oh." Now Mr. Greenblat is even more confused, probably sensing that there is some major girl stuff going down. The beam of light disappears again as he considers my fate.

Suddenly Mrs. Greenblat's voice cuts through the darkness. "Oh for goodness sakes, Mitchell! Leave the girl alone! She's not a prowler. Michael, are you just going to let her sit there all night?"

There is some shuffling as Mr. Greenblat goes back to the house, the screen door slams again, and then there is the sound of branches protesting as someone makes his way up to the tree house. I rub my cheeks, dry my eyes the best I can and hope I don't look as terrible as I feel.

I'm not surprised when Michael's face appears in the opening that acts as a doorway.

"Hey."

"Hey."

He pulls himself up, dropping a bag of Twizzlers between us as he sits.

"Want a Twizzler?"

"Okay."

We sit in silence, pulling twists of red licorice out of the bag, one by one. The little tree house smells so strongly of strawberries that it's making me dizzy.

Eventually, Michael says, "I didn't know you were coming."

"Neither did I."

"So, is everything okay?" He looks worried, like he really doesn't want to know the answer.

"No," I say, and I try to explain, but everything comes out all squeaky. Soon I'm sobbing (like with snot and everything) and Michael is patting my shoulder. And I think, I hate my mom and I hate Bill — but I could very well love Michael Greenblat.

After a disgusting sobfest that makes Denise look dainty, Michael tries to wrap his head around the situation.

"So, your dad's in town?"

"Yes."

"And he didn't know you existed?"

"Yes."

"Whoa."

"I know."

"And you thought he was here to see you, but—"

"It was his nephew, yes."

"And the nephew is in the baseball tournament?"

"Yes."

Michael chews on his licorice for a moment. "Do you want to know who he is?"

"The kid?"

"Your cousin, yeah."

"No," I say. Then I think about it for a minute. "I don't know, maybe."

"I bet we can figure out who it is. There's only one baseball tournament, and it's tomorrow. I'm going to be there. Remember I told you about it?"

"Right." I vaguely remember this. Of course, back then it was just a day of baseball games that I barely considered attending. Now it was a day of baseball games at which one of the players was my secret cousin. Very different situations.

"Well, if you do want to come, it starts at nine and goes until four." As an afterthought, he adds, "There's going to be hotdogs at lunch."

Great, I think. I'll have to see the man who didn't know he was my father, and my secret cousin, but at least there will be hotdogs.

"There's one more thing," I say. "Bill mentioned this other guy, Jack Handover. He made it sound like my mom dumped him for Jack, but Jack didn't write in her yearbook or anything."

I don't mention the message from "J." I already feel crazy.

"When did they break up?"

"Just after graduation, sometime in July," I say. I don't know this for sure, but I can do the math. It's not hard to subtract nine months from my birthday, which is in March. I'm glad it's too dark for Michael to see my cheeks, which feel like they're flaming red.

It's not a secret that my mom got pregnant and had a baby right after high school. I know I shouldn't be ashamed of where I come from, and it's not my fault my parents weren't more careful, but Michael's family is so proper and did everything in the usual order. I wonder what his mother really thinks of me and my messed-up family.

Michael flips through the yearbook. "This is her grade eleven yearbook," he says.

"So?"

"So, you said they broke up after graduation. You need to look at the grade twelve yearbook. Maybe there will more about Jack in there."

"Michael, you're a genius!"

I can't believe I didn't think of that myself. I guess my brain is too full to really work things out properly.

Eventually, Michael's mom comes to find us. I'm so tired out from all the crying, I can barely move.

"Why don't you two come inside? You can stay for a while longer, Clarissa, but I think you should call your mom."

"We're coming," Michael says.

I look at him through sore eyes, raw from crying. "I can't talk to her yet."

"Aren't you going home?"

I try to imagine walking through the door and pretending nothing's happened, but it's like trying to think of one song when you're singing another: impossible.

"Can't I sleep out here?" Even as I say it, I know what the answer will be.

Michael hesitates. "I don't think my mom would like that. She likes you and everything, but . . ."

"I know." I'm sorry I asked.

"I'm sure we can give you a ride home. I can come with you, if you want."

"Okay."

We climb out of the tree house and go into Michael's house, where his mother is waiting for us with two glasses of water. I don't know what he says to her. I'm so tired my ears are buzzing. But the next thing I know, we're getting into the car and driving the few blocks to my place.

Michael holds my hand the whole time, letting go only when I get out of the car.

***

I stumble into the house, feeling like the walking dead. I can hear the TV downstairs. Mom and Doug call up, and I make a noise that must sound somewhat normal, because neither of them asks me what's wrong or comes upstairs. Only Suzy is there to witness my misery, snuffling at my feet with her cold nose.

"Don't you start," I mutter, refusing to stop and pet her. I am not ready to forgive her for peeing in the living room and getting me in trouble.

No one in the history of the world has ever felt as tired as I do now. I find the phone and crawl into bed with it, fully clothed, stopping only to take off my shoes.

I am about to call Benji, when I remember how he told me he was busy and left me to search for my father alone. I didn't think it was possible to feel any lower, but that betrayal, as minor as it seems, feels like one more welt on my already bruised and battered heart.

I let the phone fall to the floor. With a jolt, I remember the photo of my parents, hiding under my pillow. I fish it out and fling it at the closet. It bounces off and clatters to the floor, much louder than I would like. I wait for Mom or Doug to call up and see what the fuss is, but the call never comes. Probably too busy being in love.

Part of me wants to find out more about Jack Handover, but I'm so tired and I don't think my brain can take any more.

All I want to do is sleep. And eventually, I do.

Tournament Day

In the morning I feel dried out. My eyes and throat are scratchy, and I drink two whole glasses of water as soon as I wake up. I take extra long in the shower, and by the time I'm done, I'm starting to feel human again. Mom is on the phone yelling about floral arrangements, so I write her a note and stick it on the fridge with a big happy face magnet. It's not the friendliest note I've ever written, but I'm not feeling very friendly at the moment. Maybe the happy face magnet will make up for it.

At Ferndale for Michael's baseball tournament. Gone all day. Back later. —C

I'm not convinced that going to the baseball tournament is the right thing to do, but I'm not ready to face my mother yet, and I have nowhere else to go.

***

At the park, I am happy to sit with the Greenblats. No one mentions my late-night tree house visit, not even the boys, which is a miracle. Mrs. Greenblat must have threatened them with something serious, like no candy or no TV. It's comforting to be surrounded by the warm, noisy tornado of Michael's family. I can just sit there in the middle of it all — the eye of the storm, a part of them but also separate. I accept a handful of sunscreen when Mrs. Greenblat goes around doling it out to everyone. "Don't forget your ears," she tells me. "My boys are always coming home with sunburned ears."

Michael must have filled his mom in on some of the details, because she is extra kind to me, giving me the biggest muffin and telling Solly and David to knock it off when they start chattering at me.

"It's okay, Mrs. G.; I don't mind."

It isn't long before she's telling me about how her neighbour's tree casts a shadow over the garden, and that this is bad news for her tomato plants. Because she is being so nice to me, and didn't kick me off her property when I showed up in the middle of the night, I try extra hard to pay attention. I nod and ask questions, but I can't help but scan the crowds for Bill. I'm not sure if I want to see him or not, but if he is here, I want to be prepared.

Because it's a tournament, there are a lot more people here than at Michael's other games. All three of the school's diamonds are being used, so six teams can play at a time. There must to be at least two hundred people here. Eventually I give up and try to concentrate on Mrs. Greenblat's gardening woes.

Michael comes to sit with us after his first game, which his team won. I think. I wasn't really concentrating. Mrs. Greenblat asks us to watch Theo while she takes Solly and David to the washroom, leaving us alone. Well, alone with Theo, who doesn't count. Theo knows maybe a hundred words, none of which are incriminating. I have discovered that I can make Theo laugh simply by bouncing my knees really slowly and then really fast. He laughs and laughs like he's never had a better time in his whole life. Making Theo laugh puts me in a much better mood.

Once his mother is out of earshot, Michael dives right in. "I think I know who your cousin is," he says, his voice low.

I can't believe how quickly he figured it out. "How?"

"I talked to some of the guys, asked about a player with the last name Davies."

"You didn't tell them—"

"That he's your cousin?" Michael looks horrified. "Of course not!"

I have a cousin. A cousin who grew up in the same town as me, maybe even went to the same school. And all this time I had no idea.

"Who is it?"

"See the visitors' bench?" Michael points to the bench that is farthest from where we're sitting. A line of boys in white pants and green baseball jerseys sits facing the diamond.

"Yes."

"Number fourteen, two from the end, the one with the red water bottle, that's him."

At first I can't look. I stare at the dusty ground by their bench, unable to look past their shoes. "Do we know him?" I ask.

"I don't. His family lives in the country, close to Hickson. He didn't go to Ferndale."

Chances are, I don't know him either. I feel relieved. It would have been way worse if it was someone I knew. "What's his name?"

"Nick."

Somehow, knowing his name gives me the courage to look up. He's just a boy, brownish hair, not too tall, my age or maybe a bit older. There is nothing special about him, except that we share the same DNA. The only difference is that Nick sees Bill from time to time. Bill has been a part of Nick's life, even if he wasn't around all the time. The truth stings.

Why Nick and not me? How would my life have been different if Bill had known about me? Surely a man who would fly across the country to see his nephew would make an effort for his very own daughter? Would he visit me? Would I go see him in Vancouver? Would he take me whale watching?

No. I can't think like that. It won't change anything.

I stare at Nick like I used to stare at Michael, wondering about him. Just then he turns and looks right at me. I look away, feeling caught in the act. I tell myself to relax, he couldn't possibly know who I am or what I was thinking. Unless Bill told him. Would Bill do that, call up his nephew and say, "guess what, you've got a cousin"?

"Do you want to meet him?" Michael asks.

"No." This I am sure about. It is enough to know who he is and that he exists.

I thought I was ready to expand my family by one member, my dad, and that did not turn out the way I planned. I'm not ready for a cousin, too.

Besides, there's Doug to think about now. I'm not about to call him Dad or anything, and I know he would never ask me to do that. But Doug is marrying my mother and is living in our house. He will probably make sure I do my chores, come to my graduation and do all the things a dad would normally do. He'll have the job but not the title.

I am gripped by a wave of sympathy for big, goofy Doug. I wonder if he knows about Jack, or that my mother cheated on my father and didn't have the decency to tell him that he had a daughter.

It was an ugly thing to do. I still have trouble believing my mother capable of it. Surely this is the kind of thing you should know before you agree to spend the rest of your life with someone.

"Do you know that man?"

Mrs. Greenblat is back, and her mom instincts are on high alert. She shades her eyes with a hand to get a better look at the man who is staring at me, trying to decide whether he is a pervert or not.

"Who?" Michael asks.

"That man, right there. He's staring over here."

I recognize Bill, but I am not about to explain who he is to Mrs. Greenblat.

"I do know him," I say. "I should probably say hello."

I don't really want to talk to Bill, but if I don't, Michael's mom might march over there and demand to know why he is staring at her family and her son's maybe-girlfriend.

"Do you want me to come?" Michael asks in a low voice.

"No, but thanks." I smile at him to prove how okay I am with the situation, and then I leave my safe, warm Greenblat cocoon to deal with the mess I have created. Bill smiles at me as I get closer, but it's tentative, like he's waiting for me to explode.

"Small world," Bill says.

"I'm not here to spy on you, if that's what you're thinking."

Bill's smile falters a little bit, and I enjoy how nervous I am making him. Last night he saw me at my worst. I don't want him to think that I am a stupid, emotional girl who bursts into tears at the drop of a hat. Bill is about to get a dose of the real Clarissa, smart mouth and all.

"Not at all. Look, I'm sorry I upset you last night. I was just so surprised."

"I know."

"Can I buy you a hotdog?"

"Okay." Even tough girls like hotdogs.

Bill and I walk over to the parking lot. Some dads have set up barbeques there and are selling hotdogs, chips, pop and juice, everything for a dollar.

"Pick whatever you want to drink," Bill says, like it's some noble gesture. As if being able to choose a free pop makes everything better. The drinks are floating in a cooler packed with ice that has already started to melt. I pluck a can of iced tea out of the icy water, which is so cold it makes my knuckles ache. Bill buys me a bag of chips, too.

He watches me as I take the hotdog. "What, no mustard?"

I shake my head, daring him to contradict me. "I like it plain or with mayonnaise."

"Whatever you like," he says.

We head back to the tree line at the edge of the school, where it's shady. It's a good place to eat lunch. The grass is dry and prickly beneath my legs.

I look over at the bleachers and spy Mrs. Greenblat watching us, a very stern expression on her face. It's nice to know she's so concerned about me. I wave at her so she knows that I'm okay and not about to be kidnapped by Bill. She waves back and visibly relaxes, sitting down and focusing on the game. I bet she'll continue to steal glances at us until I make my way back to the bleachers.

"So," Bill says, but he doesn't finish the sentence. Instead, he waits for me to say something. I take a few big bites of my hotdog and chew really slowly, in no hurry to talk. Let him sweat it out for a bit. Turns out Bill is the kind of man who doesn't like uncomfortable silences. He's the first one to break.

"You're what, thirteen? Fourteen? Heading into grade nine in the fall?"

"I want you to tell me about Jack Handover," I say.

Bill is taken aback, like I just threw him a wicked curveball. "Look, I shouldn't have brought him up. It wasn't my place."

"Well, you did, so now you owe it to me to tell me about him." I am cold and unrelenting. Bill Davies has seen me cry, and now he will see how tough I can be.

"Did you talk to your mother yet?"

"I want to hear what you have to say."

"Look, I really think we should just sit down with your mother and talk stuff out. I was actually going to track her down today, after the tournament."

"She won't want to talk to you."

"She doesn't have much of a choice." Bill sounds serious, but I'm not about to let that deter me.

"Don't change the subject. Tell me about Jack Handover."

Bill cracks open his can of Coke and downs it in one gulp. It's a lame attempt to buy himself time. "This is the strangest conversation I have ever had."

I have been very good at keeping calm, but my anger is back. It flares hot and ferocious, and I explode, words rushing out of my mouth, hot and angry. "How do you think I feel? Up until this summer I never thought of you, *ever*." I enjoy the way this makes Bill flinch. "Then you appear, back in town, and I find out that not only did you not even know I existed, but apparently my mother had another boyfriend.

How do I know Jack isn't my father?" My voice breaks just slightly on Jack's name, almost blowing my cover. Curse you, feelings! You're going to ruin everything!

Bill takes off his sunglasses, so he can look me in the eye. He hesitates, like he wants to touch me, but thinks better of it. "Clarissa, I'm sorry if I made you think that. I'm obviously your dad; I can tell by just looking at you."

He's right. There is a striking family resemblance. I bet all the people here at the tournament are thinking, "Oh look, there's a father and daughter having lunch on a nice summer day," like it's no big deal, like it's something Bill and I do all the time. If only they knew the truth.

"I should never have mentioned Jack; it was a dumb ass move on my part. I do a lot of dumb-ass things. I'm sure your mother has told you all about them." Bill smiles ruefully when he says this, as if being cute and self-deprecating can make it all better.

I do not return his smile. "No, actually. She never mentions you." I say this with all the cool disdain I can muster after my eruption.

"Well, that's probably for the better."

"I wish I never met you."

Maybe that's hitting below the belt, but I can't help myself. I want him to feel as awful as I felt last night. I'm not even sure I mean it.

Discovering your dad is not a reformed deadbeat, pining after his long-lost daughter, but is actually just an average guy who had no clue, is pretty bad. But at least I only had a few weeks to build up our reunion in my mind. That's not such a long time. I could have spent years imagining our perfect reunion, only to be even more disappointed than I am now. What if I got some crazy idea in my head that

I wanted my birth father to be at my wedding, only to discover that he was a big loser? Then my life would be like some weird, twisted version of *Mamma Mia!*, but with no singing and no handsome birth father.

"I bet you do," Bill says sadly.

We're both finished eating, and it feels like there is nothing left to say. I stand and wipe my hands on my shorts. "Thanks for the hotdog."

"Where are you going?"

"I should go back to my friends," I say.

Bill puts his sunglasses back on, stands, and then we hang out by the tree for a minute, not sure what to do next. "We're not done here. I still need to talk to your mother. Maybe we can—"

"Don't bother," I say, but I stop. Maybe it would be easiest to walk away and erase everything that happened this week. No one knows the whole story except me, Bill, Michael and maybe Mrs. Greenblat. I could lie and tell Benji I never went to the Lilac Motel. He'd be so relieved about not having to go there that he'd probably drop the subject of finding my father completely. I could forget all about running around like a maniac, trying to track Bill down. And after a while the details would become fuzzy, and this whole week would become a hazy memory. But he's being so nice, I'm not sure what to do.

"Can one of you please explain to me what the hell is going on here?"

As I was saying, it *might* have been easiest to walk away, but unfortunately my mother decided to bring me a lunch. Now she's standing in front of us, clutching a paper bag so hard her knuckles have turned white. I never should have told her where the tournament was.

"Annie," Bill says. "Long time no see."

"What the hell is going on?"

"Calm down."

Uh-oh. You never tell Annie Delaney to calm down. You would think an ex-boyfriend would remember that.

"Don't tell me to calm down. I come looking for my daughter and find her sitting with you? You have ten seconds to explain what is going on before I completely lose it."

My mom doesn't lose her temper often. When she gets angry she tends to get cold and mean. Now she looks about ready to explode. People are starting to notice.

"*She* found me! Imagine my surprise when some kid — some *teenager* — waltzes up and says, 'Hi, I'm your daughter.' If anyone has some explaining to do, it's you."

I don't like the way he calls me "some kid." Not that I was ever on his side, but I'm feeling less sorry about the royal smackdown he's about to get from my mother.

"I don't have to explain anything to you. It was years ago. We were over. You moved away. The end."

"That's bull, Annie, and you know it. You could have got ahold of me if you wanted to. They have phones in Vancouver, you know. And the internet. Were you just never going to tell me?"

A small crowd has gathered, and pretty soon there are more people watching us than the baseball game.

"And what was she missing, exactly? What would you have offered?"

Bill tries another tactic. Maybe he's noticed the crowd and decided he doesn't want to be labelled public enemy number one. "Let's go someplace else to talk about this. I don't really want to put Clarissa through this."

So he does remember my name.

"Don't you tell me what my daughter has and hasn't been through. You spend five minutes with her and you think you know what's best for her?"

In some ways, I feel like I'm watching a play: Shakespeare in the Park, or a trashy, small-town version of it. I almost forget the person they're arguing about is me.

"What's going on here? Annie, are you okay?"

Doug appears, carrying three ice cream cones. I could faint from embarrassment. The Shakespeare-in-the-Park version of my life has now officially become a soap opera. Behind me, people are whispering, relishing the drama of it all.

"Who's that?"

"The boyfriend."

"And the other guy?"

"Her ex. That's their kid."

Mom looks like she might be sick. Either that, or she's steeling herself to attack Bill. "Doug, just give me a minute. Take Clarissa and go home. I'll meet you there."

Doug doesn't look convinced, possibly because Bill has started ranting. "You don't get to decide what did and didn't happen, Annie! You tell her I'm not a bad guy; that you're the one who cheated on me. You were messing around with Jack for weeks before you had the guts — no, the decency — to break it off with me. You know, if it wasn't for the resemblance, I'd demand a paternity test. Given her age, I'd say she has a fifty-fifty chance of being his kid."

The rest happens so quickly, it takes a moment for my brain to catch up with what I'm seeing. Doug shoves all three ice cream cones into my hands, saying, "Hold these."

Then he steps between Mom and Bill, hands out, like a peacekeeper. "I get that you're mad, Bill, but let's all take it down a notch."

But Bill is too angry. "Who do you think you are?" He lunges forward, arm spring-loaded and ready to fly.

"Don't!"

The scream that comes out of Mom's throat is ragged and demanding, like one of those ancient Greek super-goddesses who can freeze people with just her voice. Or maybe I made that up. I don't pay a lot of attention in history. She throws herself at Bill, wrapping herself around his arm. He looks at his fist, as if he's not sure what to do with the human mitten that has attached itself to him. I'm so shocked, I don't even move to wipe the chocolate ice cream that is running down my hand.

A Totally
Weird Day

Not surprisingly, we are all asked to leave the tournament.

Mom calms down enough to agree to sit and talk with Bill.

"I want to come," I say.

"I don't think that's a good idea," Doug says, steering me in the opposite direction, toward the parking lot. "We need to give those two some time to talk things out. They have a lot to catch up on."

I am incredulous. "And you're just going to let her go with him? A violent man like that? Aren't you mad?"

"I'm mad at myself for letting the situation escalate like that."

"He was going to hit you!"

Doug looks stern. "And I might have hit him back, if your mother hadn't stepped in." He shakes his head, clearly disappointed in himself. "No matter what happens, it is never okay to sock someone in the face, okay, Clarissa?"

I try hard not to roll my eyes. "Well, obviously. How long do you think this talk will take?"

"An hour, maybe two."

"I hate that they're talking about me and I'm not allowed to be there."

"They're trying to figure out what's best for you."

"Without even consulting me? Don't I get a say in what I want?"

Doug sighs. "You know what I want? To go bowling. It'll help take our mind off things."

So we end up at Shake, Rock 'n' Bowl. The only other people at the bowling alley are some kids at a birthday party. They're wearing party hats and shrieking away in the kids' lane, the one with the bright yellow bumpers lining the gutters. One of the kids has tied balloons to his wrists and keeps jumping off the chairs, like maybe he thinks he'll actually fly. Kids can be so dumb.

Doug and I play one full game, but my heart isn't in it. I let him win, and then I go see if Charity is working at the snack bar, promising to bring back fries. Sure enough, there she is, leaning over the counter, reading a magazine, slowly dipping her finger in and out of a giant cup of Coke.

"Hey, Charity."

Charity is thrilled to see me. She smiles, and her eyes light up. I am reminded of how star quality really isn't something you can fake. No wonder Benji has a crush on her. "Clarissa! Thank god you're here. I was just about to die of boredom. What's up?"

What's up? My mom's getting married on Sunday, and my long-lost dad just about got in a fist fight with her fiancé. That's what up. But enough people in this town already know my business, so what I say is, "Nothing much."

"Nothing much here, either. Except the showcase, of course." Charity is a bona-fide actress, dedicated to her craft. She does commercials in addition to starring in all the local theatre productions. She even had two lines in a TV show once.

"Dean is the best thing that ever happened to us," she goes on. "He's the real deal, you know? I mean he's studying theatre in the city and seeing all sorts of really groundbreaking shows . . . He's really turned things around."

"Yeah, Benji seems to think so. He talks about Dean the way he used to talk about you."

"What do you mean?"

"You were his theatre idol; he used to go around quoting everything you said. Now Dean is the one he can't stop talking about. No offence."

Charity laughs. "None taken. Dean is all any of us are talking about. Have you met him?"

"Once. At the mall."

Charity leans over the counter as if she's about to share a secret. "Cute, right?"

"Isn't he a little old for you?"

"Not really. Three years isn't that big a difference."

"Do you think he's interested in you?"

Charity shrugs. "I can't tell yet. But let's just say I've started to wear mascara to rehearsal."

I can't help but laugh. When Charity wants something, she usually gets it. Poor Teen Dream Dean doesn't stand a chance. I wonder if Benji knows. He can't seriously think he stands a chance against Dean, can he?

"Come on, wouldn't you?" she asks.

"Nope. He's all yours."

"Oh right, I forgot you're taken. You only have eyes for that baseball player."

"His name is Michael, and I am not *taken*. Mostly I watch him play baseball," I admit.

"Sounds like love to me. Can you even name a single baseball team?"

"A real one?"

"A professional team, yes."

"The Toronto Blue Jays."

"Doesn't count. Everyone knows them. Name another one."

I think of all the times Michael has given me recaps of "incredible" games that I've missed. Usually, I just nod and think about how adorable he looks when he's excited, so no actual team names come to mind. I take a stab in the dark. "The Red . . . Wings?"

"That's hockey."

"The Red . . . Sox?"

"Lucky guess."

"Fine. So I only go to baseball games because Michael's there. Isn't that what people do where they're—"

"Dating?" Charity finishes, grinning wickedly at me. She's enjoying this way too much.

Then, abruptly, she changes the subject. "Hey, can I ask you a question?"

"Sure."

"Is everything okay with Benji?"

"Why?"

"Maybe it's nothing, but he seems a little off lately."

"Off, how?"

"Sort of distant. Like he's hiding something."

Before I thought I was being extra-sensitive because of everything else that's going on in my life, but now I'm not so sure. If Charity's picked up on Benji's weird behaviour, that means something is definitely up with him. "What sort of things have you noticed?" I ask.

"Little things. Like usually a bunch of us take break together, go and talk to Dean, ask him about what school is like, but lately he hangs back and pretends to read his script."

"How do you know he's pretending?"

"Because I've caught him staring at me a few times. And yesterday Dean offered to drive me home after rehearsal, and when I told Benji I couldn't walk with him, he sort of shut down. Then this morning he barely said hello."

For Benji to not be overly polite is alarming. "Weird," I say.

"I know," Charity agrees. "Does Benji ever talk to you about girls? Like a crush?"

"No, but I don't talk about boys much, either. He embarrasses too easily."

"And you two never . . . ?" Charity trails off, waiting for me to fill in the blank.

"Never what?"

"You know, dated."

"God, no!"

"Not even a kiss?"

"Never. I don't think of him like that. He's like my brother."

"And you think he feels the same way about you?"

"I know he does."

"Okay. Did you ever think—" Charity stops and takes a long sip of her drink.

"What?"

Charity continues, "Never mind. It's none of my business. I feel kinda bad, picking the poor guy apart. Can't a person have a few bad days? The bottom line is, the Benj is a straight-up cool guy, and we should cut him some slack."

"If you say so."

"I do."

"Okay." Charity really is great. It's hard to believe I used to hate her guts. On a whim, I ask, "Hey, what are you doing tomorrow at three?"

"I'm free, I think."

"Want to come to an end-of-summer barbeque at my house?"

She looks genuinely pleased. "Clarissa, I would *love* that! Thank you so much!"

I feel good about inviting her. I don't mention that the barbeque is directly following my mother's wedding. I'm not really in the mood to explain it.

Charity and I haven't really bonded, even though we've hung out a few times together with Benji. But we're all going to be at the same school now, so we're likely to see each other a lot more. Plus, Benji really likes her, so I might as well put a little effort into it, especially if she ends up as his girlfriend. Though if Dean is an option, things don't look so good for Benji.

Cripes! Listen to me going on about bonding and effort! Am I turning into Doug?

"Am I going to see you tonight?" she asks.

"What's tonight?"

"There's a party! Didn't Benji tell you? I told him to bring you!"

It hurts too much to admit that, no, Benji did *not* tell me about this mysterious party, so I play forgetful. "Oh right, I remember something about a party now. Where is it?"

"My place, any time after eight. Sort of a back-to-school thing, mostly for Gaslighters and some friends from school. Only cool people — you'll like them, I promise."

Normally I wouldn't jump at the chance to hang out with a group of needy actors connected by joke after inside joke, but the alternative is my mom's idea of a bachelorette party: movies and manicures with Denise. It's something we've done a hundred times, and the last thing I want to do is spend quality time with my mom the liar.

"I'll be there."

***

Doug and I play one more game, even though I am dying to be anywhere else but here. He keeps trying to engage me in conversation, which is annoying. I know he's trying to keep me distracted, but it's no use. What I really want is to be left alone with my thoughts. I can't take back the fact that I know Bill. I have met him, and we have talked. As much as I would like to be mad at him, it's hard to stay angry at someone who honestly didn't know I exist.

It's my mom I'm really mad at. She's the one who knew the truth and kept it from me.

Doug keeps checking his phone.

"Any word?" I ask.

Doug shoves his phone in his pocket, like he got caught doing something bad. Does he seriously think I can't see him checking it every two minutes? "Not yet."

"Doug, this is nice of you and everything, but do you think you could take me home? I just want to be by myself."

"Of course, C-Money. I'll just let Annie know we're headed home."

It doesn't bother me when Doug uses the word home anymore. It's been bumped off the list of things that upset me right now.

As we leave, I wave to Charity, who gives me a wink and

says "Byyyye," in this sing-songy way that lets me know I'm in for some fun tonight.

"Your mother says she'll be home soon. Do you want to play a game or watch a movie?"

"I don't need a babysitter," I say. Then, because Doug has been so nice, I add, "I'm probably going to take a nap, anyway."

"You got it, CLD. If you want to talk, I'll be in the back-yard. I need to do some grooming before The Big Day." Doug uses air quotes around the words "The Big Day," then smiles like a kid. I guess boys get just as excited about wed-dings as girls do. Even when the girl they're marrying turns out to be a liar.

"It doesn't bother you? That she lied to him?"

"It was a long time ago."

"Or that she cheated on her boyfriend? That could be you in a few years."

Doug doesn't even flinch. "We all do stupid things when we're teenagers."

Not me, I think. I will never be that stupid.

Party Day

When she opens the door, Charity cries, "You came!" and pulls me inside. Then she turns to the small crowd and says, "Look everyone, it's Clarissa! She came!"

In movies, parties are always held in beautiful houses packed full of beautiful people who are drunk, dancing and making out all over the place. Someone gets humiliated, something expensive gets broken and someone always pukes. Maybe this is true of other high school parties, but it is not so at Charity's.

There are maybe ten people hanging around in her living room. Some are squished on the couches, and others sort of loiter behind, holding pop or beer cans or handfuls of chips. On the coffee table are two bowls of snacks, and a pizza box is open on the island that divides the living room from the kitchen. Music is playing in the background, but it isn't even loud enough to recognize the song. I've been to birthday parties for seven-year-olds that were wilder.

"Let's get you a drink," Charity says, and she leads me into the kitchen, still grasping my wrist for some reason. Maybe she thinks I'll get lost on my way across the living room? People nod and smile as we pass. Some of them I recognize as people from the show Charity and Benji did in the spring, but some are total strangers.

"Now there is beer, and some coolers, but you don't have to drink them if you don't want to. I have lots of pop, too."

Denise let me try her beer once, which tasted like warm, strained garbage. No thanks. I pick up a bottle of something pink and fruity looking. "What's this?"

"That's a watermelon cooler."

"I'll have this."

"Are you sure? It has alcohol in it," Charity looks uncertain, as if she's just realized I'm only fourteen.

"Definitely."

It's not like I've never had alcohol before. At New Year's Mom will put a splash of champagne in my orange juice. She probably wouldn't be pleased about the cooler, but she has lost the right of telling me what I can and cannot do. After this week, knowing what I know now, her opinion is just something for me to consider. It is no longer the final word.

So what if I have one pretty-looking pink drink? I'm not going to get drunk and do something stupid. I'm not a stereotype in a teen movie.

"Well, help yourself!"

The drink is good: syrupy but with a slightly bitter, almost metallic aftertaste. I don't feel any cooler drinking it, but it's nice to have something to hold on to. Aside from Charity, no one here really knows me, which is kind of a relief. No one thinks, "oh, look at the poor, fatherless child," or, "isn't that the girl whose mother had breast cancer?" The only thing interesting about me tonight is that I am a mysterious stranger. I can say anything or be anyone, including an underage cooler-drinker. Unless Benji (that traitor) shows up, I am a blank slate.

I take a long swallow, for courage, then wander up to the friendliest-looking group in the room. Three girls, all smiles, hanging out on a couch. I don't recognize any of them, but they are all drinking the same watermelon cooler as me. At the very least we can talk about that.

"Hey."

"Hey."

"I'm Clarissa."

"Rachel."

"Kiera."

"Jess."

I'll never remember all those names. It doesn't help that they're dressed alike and two of them have hair the exact same shade of brown with the same bangs. The only difference is that one of them clearly uses a flat iron and the other does not.

"How do you know Charity?" one of them asks.

"Through my friend Benji," I say.

One of the girls — maybe Rachel? — smiles and nods. "I know Benji. Really sweet, kind of shy. We were both in *The Wizard*," she explains to the matching-hair girls, who now wear matching blank expressions.

"Is he cute?" one of them asks.

"Yeah, but he's not your type. Besides, he's, like, thirteen," says Rachel.

"Fourteen," I correct.

The girl pouts. "Too bad. I like older guys. Are you dating anyone, Clarissa?"

"Yes," I say, thinking, what the heck? I don't think Michael will mind. We basically are. "He's a baseball player."

"A good one?"

"Pretty good."

"God, I can't wait for school to start. This has been the longest summer ever."

"Poor Jess has spent the whole summer babysitting," Rachel says to me, patting Jess on the knee.

"Like, actual baby babysitting," Jess says. "Diapers-and-screaming-and-crying babysitting. I never thought I'd say this, but even geography with Nadinski is better."

The other girls protest.

"He's the worst," Rachel says.

"Do you go to Sir John A.?" Kiera asks.

"I start next week," I say.

"Well, pray you don't get Nadinski," she says.

"He teaches grade nine geography and grade eleven history," Rachel explains. "He reads from his notes and doesn't take questions. It's a wonder no one has died of boredom in his class."

"Lowell is okay," says Kiera, "but you really want to be in Ms. Singh's class. She's the best."

"The best," Jess agrees.

"If you end up with Mr. Cochrane for math, always do the homework. He gets you to hand it in randomly for marks."

"Never use the bathrooms near the music room, they're always out of toilet paper."

"And bring your lunch if you can. The caf food is disgusting."

I nod after each of their suggestions, making mental notes so I can pass them on to Michael and Mattie. And maybe Benji, if he decides he wants to hang out again.

Charity is a great host. She flits around the room, inserting herself into pockets of conversation for a minute or two, then moving on to the next group.

"Hey, Charity, is Dean coming?"

"I invited him."

A few girls giggle.

"Do you think he'll show?"

"I don't see why not."

A girl who has been sitting slightly apart from my new friends, the Couch Girls, frowns and says, "Isn't he in university? He's too old for this kind of party."

Charity takes mock offence to that statement and turns up the music. "What kind of party?" she says. "An awesome party?" Then she pulls the Naysayer up off the couch, and they dance around a bit. It's pretty lame, but also kind of silly, and soon I'm giggling, too. Charity sees me and throws an arm around my shoulders, and then all three of us are sort of giggle-swaying to a song I've never heard of, but all of a sudden really, really, like.

"What's this song?" I ask.

"You mean you don't know? It's on the radio, like, every five seconds," says the Naysayer.

Charity just laughs, but not in a mean way. "Clarissa, I love you! It's like you live in this vacuum."

She places her hands on my shoulders and says, "Let me teach you. I will guide you in the ways of music and the world."

I slip free of her hands, laughing. "Maybe I live in a vacuum, but you live in a bubble of jazz hands and show tunes."

The Naysayer is delighted. "So true! What's your name again?"

"Clarissa."

She smiles at me and says, "I'm Megan."

Charity bounces over to her music player and selects a Broadway tune I've never heard before.

"Welcome to the bubble!" she cries. The song must be from a Gaslight Players show, because four or five other people pop up, and they all perform it — or the parts they remember — singing really loudly, while bumping into each other in exaggerated, half-forgotten choreography.

"Are you a Gaslighter?" I ask Megan, trying not to choke on the name, which is still lame even after a third of a watermelon cooler.

"No, I go to school with Charity and some of the others."

"Me, neither." I am feeling warmed by my new kinship with Megan (and possibly the cooler, which tastes less tinny and more delicious). "Is it just me, or is Gaslighter a weird thing to call yourself?"

To my delight, Megan laughs. "Totally. It sounds like a kind of bad fart joke a nine-year-old would tell, right? I mean, *Gas*lighter? Come on!"

It is a relief to hang out with someone who finally gets it. "Exactly!"

Megan holds her own cooler up. "Cheers to that," she says. We clink bottles, then drink some more.

The song has ended, and the Gaslighters are cheering and hugging and giving each other high-fives. Charity changes the music but keeps the volume up.

I am almost done my cooler when Benji shows up. He's dressed up again: black jeans, a new skinny t-shirt and — *oh my god* — is that *product* in his hair? It feels like I haven't seen him in ages, and all I want to do is give him a big hug. When was the last time we hugged? Hugging is great! I forget that I am angry with him and run forward to greet him with open arms. "BENJI!"

We collide, my teeth knocking the side of his ear some-how.

"Whoops, sorry!" My body is starting to feel like it belongs to someone else. It's getting harder to control it.

"What are you doing here? Are you drinking?"

"Why so many questions?" I say. "Aren't you glad to see me?"

"Your mom is going to kill you."

"Unlikely, she has some ecks . . . some ess . . . some . . . 'splaining to do of her own." I've never realized how tricky it is to pronounce the word explaining before. Benji is trying not to smile, I can tell.

What a good friend, always worried about not hurting people's feelings and doing the right thing. I hug him again, and this time nothing is bumped. "I'm so happy to see you. I miss you."

Behind me, Charity laughs. "She's only had one, can you believe it?"

I feel Benji's shoulders stiffen. "You shouldn't have given her one at all," he says. "We're underage."

Charity waves this off, and then she puts one arm around each of us, walking us into the party. "Don't worry, nothing will happen. It's better to experiment in a safe environment with responsible adults."

"Yeah, Benji. I'm fine," I say, patting his shoulder.

"What adults?" Benji asks. Then he looks at my hand. "Clarissa, are you petting me?"

Charity gasps, mock-hurt. "Um, me? Megan? Bennet?"

"You're not exactly adults," Benji points out. Why is he being such a downer?

"I'm not a downer—" Benji says.

Uh-oh, did I say that aloud? I really am losing control of my body.

"Relax. Dean will be here soon, and he's *definitely* a man." Charity smiles seductively, and behind her someone giggles.

"I can't believe you're drinking," Benji whispers.

"What do you care? You didn't even tell me about the party. I had to pretend I knew all about it when Charity asked. She seemed to think you had invited me."

"I was going to."

"But you didn't. And you abandoned me yesterday to go to the mall with Dean."

"I didn't abandon you."

"You said you had stuff to do for the show and then got sundaes."

Benji has nothing more to say.

"What is going on? You've been acting weird!" I try to lower my voice, but it's harder than I remember. Isn't whispering a natural instinct, like breathing? Why is it suddenly so difficult? "I needed you! There is some serious stuff going on, and you're never there. Why are you never there?"

Benji grabs my arm and leads me to a corner away from everyone else. He does it very gently, even though I can tell by the tension in his jaw that he is really, really angry. If this were a cartoon, smoke would be coming out of his ears, and maybe his nose. And maybe his eyes would be bugging out a little, and his face would be all red. Imagine if we *were* cartoons? Charity would be all hair and smiles, and Dean would have an enormous head with shiny teeth. I can totally see them both in my head, and I hold back my laughter because Benji is so mad.

"What's so funny?"

I guess I was giggling out loud.

"Cartoons," I giggle. "Dean has such a big head."

Benji looks around. "What are you talking about? Dean's not even here."

"Yet," I say, holding onto some of Charity's enthusiasm. "Dean's not here *yet*."

"Clarissa, is everything okay? Did something happen with," Benji lowers his voice, "Bill?"

"Stupid Bill. Stupid Annie, stupid Bill, stupid Clarissa. Stupid, stupid, stupid."

Benji takes the empty bottle from me and holds on to my elbow. To be fair, I was flailing a bit. "What's stupid? What happened?"

I really do want to tell him, but where to start? In my head, I wade through all the surprising and painful and angry conversations I've had since last night, and I am overwhelmed. The giggles are gone; all my words are gone.

"Clarissa? Are you okay?"

I am trapped in my own head. I'm not sure I could get my mouth to work if I wanted to. The music is too loud, and the air in the room feels too close. It's hard to breathe it in. Actually I can't remember the last time I took a breath at all. What if I'm suffocating? How do you make your lungs work?

"Are you going to be sick?"

I'm too busy remembering how to breathe to answer.

"Let's go outside."

***

It isn't much cooler outside, but at least the air feels like it's moving a bit. After the hot, noisy room, it's a relief to be swallowed up by the dark night. I can feel my heart and my lungs calming down.

"Better?"

Benji's voice sounds a million times louder out here. I wince and cover my ears.

"Stop yelling."

"I'm not yelling. You're drunk."

"I am not drunk!"

Am I drunk? Mostly I feel giddy and a bit silly. Most people wouldn't call me a silly person, but I've had silly moments before. It doesn't mean I'm drunk. Plus, my sense of hearing feels heightened. I can hear all of the night noises around me clear as day. Cricket, crunch of gravel, TV show in the distance. I bet if I concentrated hard enough, I could decipher exactly what TV show it is, like a superhero. If I'm so drunk, then why do I have superhero hearing? Benji is wrong.

"I am not drunk," I repeat. "I have, like, supersonic hearing right now. If only you could hear what I hear, you would know I am not drunk."

"Clarissa, you ran across a room to hug me."

"What, so I can't hug people now? Hugging is a sign of drunkenness?"

"You *never* hug people."

"You never wear hair gel."

Immediately Benji's hand flies up to his hair.

"Or that t-shirt. I've never even seen that t-shirt. Since when do you have clothes I don't see?"

"Dean picked it out—"

"Oh, *Dean*, of course."

"—when we were at the mall."

"Right, the mall, when you ditched me."

"I didn't ditch you! I told you I had stuff to do!"

Benji's voice is getting higher and higher, which means he's mad. Good. I'm mad, too.

"So shopping with Dean is more important than helping me track down my father? Or deal with my mother's shotgun wedding?"

Benji looks away and says quietly, "Stuff is going on with me, too, you know."

If it wasn't for my super-hearing, I probably would have missed it.

"*What* stuff? Why won't you tell me? It's like you've been avoiding me all summer! And I happen to know you've been avoiding Charity, too."

I must have hit the nail on the head, because Benji stands up to go. "I'm not talking to you like this; you're drunk."

"I had one cooler," I say.

"Did you have dinner?"

"I can't remember." When was the last time I ate anything other than some chips? It feels like I've been at this party for hours. My mouth is dry and sticky at the same time. How is that possible?

"You should get some water."

I can hear the disappointment in Benji's voice, which smothers any flicker of giddiness, alcohol-induced or not, I have left. His mother was killed by a drunk driver when he was four years old. This was before I knew him. I don't remember how I found out. My mom must have told me, or maybe it was one of those things you just know by living in a place and absorbing things. We never talk about it, although he has made a vow never to drink, and I know his mother is the reason why.

"Well, excuse me for wanting to lighten up and have a good time like a normal person." Now I'm the one standing and walking away. I trip on the leg of a lounge chair and fumble a few times with the latch on the screen door. The alcohol may have given me supersonic hearing, but it has made my fingers feel fat and clumsy.

Inside, more people have arrived. They're everywhere,

standing, dancing a little or just talking. The music is louder, and Charity has turned off the overhead light and switched on a few lamps for atmosphere. This feels more like the parties in the movies, although I doubt this crowd will break expensive dishes or play complicated drinking games involving ping-pong tables.

I worm through the bodies, apologizing every three seconds as I seem to bump into everyone. No one seems to care. One guy even says, "Hey, no worries! I've been trying to get cute girls to bump into me all night!"

That is the lamest thing I have ever heard, but I hear myself laugh anyway, so I guess the alcohol must still be working.

I look for someone I know: Charity, the Couch Girls, my new friend Megan. Somehow, despite all the people, I feel lonelier now than I did when it was just a handful of us. I don't want to be a mysterious stranger anymore. I want someone to be excited to see me, someone who knows who I am and can tell I've had a bad day — scratch that, bad week — just by looking at me. I wish I had invited Michael.

Maybe I can call him, tell him to come over. Charity's house is not that far, he could walk. He'd probably be thrilled that I was the one inviting him somewhere for a change. I could introduce him to the Couch Girls. Now if only I could find the phone. Since Charity is nowhere to be found, I'm going to have to hunt for it. I look in all the usual places — end tables, the fireplace mantle, kitchen counter — but all I find is the empty cradle tucked beside a coffee maker in the kitchen. Someone's taken the phone someplace else.

Charity didn't bother giving me a full tour, so I wander around, peeking into rooms. Bathroom, office, mudroom.

No phone. I head upstairs, noticing how nice and soft the carpet feels under my grubby summer toes. Hmmm. It's also very white. Maybe we aren't supposed to go up here? Oh well. No one is yelling at me to come back down. Plus, what if there is an emergency? There really should be a phone on the main level. If anything, Charity should thank me for looking out for the safety of her guests.

It's quiet and dark upstairs. I can't find the light switch for the hallway, so I walk very slowly along the wall, feeling my way through the darkness, peering into shadowy rooms.

Suddenly the hallway is flooded with light so bright, it's painful. I close my eyes then open them slowly, so I can adjust to the brightness. Benji is at one end of the hall, frowning at me.

"Clarissa? You shouldn't be up here — Charity?"

Whatever Benji was going to say, is cut off by the sight of Charity and Dean on the window seat at the other end of the hall. Charity is sitting on Dean's lap, blinking at us. He has one hand on her thigh and the other is lost in the wild tumble of her hair. They both look dishevelled and flushed, but not all that embarrassed. Not nearly as embarrassed as I am.

Charity recovers first, adjusting the neckline of her shirt, which has been twisted over one shoulder. "Hey, guys? Do you mind heading back downstairs? This floor is off limits."

"Sorry, I was just looking for the phone, but I don't need it. Sorry!"

I can't get out of there quickly enough, but Benji is two steps ahead of me. He's already booked it out of there and is nowhere to be seen. I hit the light switch, and Charity and Dean disappear, hidden once more from prying eyes. Tiny spots of light pulse in my eyes, and I pray that my clumsy, half-drunk feet won't trip me up as I rush down the stairs in the dark. As much as I wish I hadn't actually seen them in action, I'm impressed with Charity's conquest. She wanted Dean, and it looks like she got him.

Downstairs, I search for Benji, but he's impossible to find. My supersonic hearing has been replaced with a ringing in my ears, and exhaustion slams into me like a wall. Home feels very far away, and the thought of walking makes me want to find a bed or a couch, or even a nice bit of floor somewhere, and sleep until morning.

What I need is a ride. But who do I call?

Mom is obviously out of the question. Doug is a possibility, but then he might get in trouble for letting me out of his sight. There is no way I can call on Mrs. Greenblat again, especially after I showed up in her tree house late last night. Plus, she'll probably smell the alcohol on my breath and, no matter how many times I tell her I just had one watermelon cooler, she will see me as a bad influence. Michael will never be allowed to see me again. There's only one person left.

Someone has left their phone on the coffee table. I'm sure they won't mind if I borrow it for one call.

Judgment Day

The price of calling Denise for a ride is listening to her rub it in my face.

"I have to say, I'm flattered you called. I mean, I'm mad as hell at you for taking off without leaving a note, and choosing tonight of all nights to start drinking. But calling me was the right thing to do."

"I'm not starting anything. I just had one cooler."

"Smart girl. One cooler, once in a while, is not such a bad thing. It's when you have two or three or four that the trouble starts. But don't tell your mother I said that. Because you really shouldn't be drinking at all. There is a reason there's a drinking age, you know."

"And I bet both of you never had a sip until your nineteenth birthdays," I say. "Like perfect little angels."

Denise doesn't answer. After a moment, she says, "I take it you're pretty mad at her."

"Yep. Are you going to tell me it's not her fault, and I can't possibly understand?"

"I wouldn't dream of it. You've got a right to be mad."

"Thank you." My head is spinning a little. I lean it against the car window, but then it smacks against the pane each time we hit a bump in the road, so I sit up.

"But I will say this: your mother didn't mean you any harm. She did what she did because she thought it was best for you. Now maybe you disagree with her, but she meant well, all right?"

I jam my teeth together to resist talking back. I guess it's too much to ask my mother's best friend to disagree with her.

"So don't go giving that woman any more grief. Today was hard, for both of you, but you've still got to live with each other."

Denise pulls into the driveway but doesn't turn off the car.

"Aren't you coming in?"

"Not tonight."

"But I thought you were going to stay over and do your nails?"

Denise shakes her head. "You two have some hashing out to do. I'll come back in the morning. Your mother is getting married tomorrow, so you do what you have to do to clear the air tonight. No one deserves all that baggage on their wedding day."

"That was almost wise."

Denise snorts, then leans over and opens the car door for me. "You're stalling. Get out of this car and make things right."

"I don't know if I can. I can't act like nothing happened, or it's no big deal."

"Well, right-ish then."

"I can't believe you're moving."

"Is that your roundabout way of telling me you're going to miss me?"

I am unable to answer, in case I start crying.

Denise clears her throat, then continues, "Next to Annie, you're the person I'm going to miss the most. You'll just have to come visit me in the big city. I'll take you shopping. But not if you don't get out of this car and talk things out with your mother."

Denise tries to smile at me, but I can see that she's holding back tears. She wags her finger at me and says, "Don't you start. If you cry, then I'll cry, and there will be enough crying tomorrow."

"What for?"

"People always cry at weddings."

"Not me."

"I bet you ten bucks you will."

"Deal."

"Great. I can't wait to say I told you so. Now, get out."

And this time I do.

* * *

Mom is waiting up for me. I brace myself for a fight, but she looks tired and small — a bundle of worn-out nerves on the couch in the living room.

"Where's Doug?" I ask.

"He's spending the night with friends. It's bad luck to see the bride before the wedding. I think the more important question is, where were you?"

"At a party."

"Where?"

"Charity's."

"And you didn't think to tell me where you were?"

"Well *you* didn't think to tell my dad that I existed, so I guess we're even."

I fully expect her to start yelling at me, but she considers me for a moment and then says, "I don't know what to say. I have a feeling no matter what I say, it won't make a difference."

"Probably not."

"So why don't you get it all off your chest?"

I look at her, waiting for the catch, but she's watching me expectantly. "Okay. Why didn't you tell him about me?"

"I didn't want to share my child with him. He wasn't for me, and I didn't want him in my life or my baby's life. By the time I found out I was pregnant, Bill had already gone to B.C. and made it clear he didn't want to speak to me, so I just . . . didn't tell him. He's not a bad person, Clarissa, but when you share a child with someone, they're in your life forever, whether you're married or not."

"Maybe you didn't want him in your life, but what about me?"

"I thought I was doing the best thing for both of us."

I'm trying to be calm, I really am, but it's those words, "the best thing," that trigger the anger in me, and I'm yelling again. "You mean the best thing for YOU. Did you know he was here visiting his nephew? Maybe he would have visited me if you'd bothered to tell him. Maybe he wasn't such a bad guy. Maybe all this time it's YOU who were the bad guy. You let me believe he was some kind of deadbeat who wouldn't want anything to do with me, but you really never gave him the chance. All this time you acted like he was the bad guy, but you broke up because *you* cheated on *him*. Then you didn't give him a chance to be my dad. You're a liar; a liar and a slut!" I want to say more, but my throat is raw. I stand there taking ragged breaths and waiting for her to say something, but she just stands there. "Don't you have anything to say?"

Mom swallows. "Ouch."

She looks so hurt it makes my heart ache, even though I'm mad at her.

"Are you mad at me because I kept you away from Bill, or because you found out I wasn't perfect?"

"Because of Bill," I say, but even as the words come out of my mouth, I'm not sure they're entirely true.

I'm mad about Bill, but the thing that has really changed is my idea of my mom. She's not the person I thought she was. In my head, she was a teenage beauty queen, the town's favourite daughter. More than that, she was my role model: a single mom running her own business and a breast cancer survivor. Those things are still true, but it's also true that she cheated on her boyfriend and didn't tell him about his daughter. Finding out that she was just as mean and stupid as some trashy teenager from a reality TV show is disappointing, embarrassing and awful all at the same time.

"I'm not perfect, and I'm sorry if that's what you believed all this time. But you must know by now that no one is perfect, baby. Bill and I were hot and cold. When we were good, things were great, but when they were bad, well, let's just say we both did things to hurt each other. It didn't end well with Bill, and I wasn't very fair to Jack, either. I know that, and I like to think that I've changed since then. You know, when people make mistakes in high school, generally their kids don't find out." Then she looks me right in the eye and adds, "I'm sorry that you did, for both of us. Nobody wants her daughter to think she's a slut."

Hearing that word repeated back to me floods me with hot shame. "I'm sorry, Mom," I blurt, walking forward into her arms. "I'm really, really sorry."

Mom hugs me carefully, letting me cry on her shoulder. "You may be sorry, but you meant it."

"No, I'm sorry! I really am!"

"I know you are. I am, too, more than you will ever know." She pulls away and brushes the tears from my cheeks with her thumbs. "Have you been missing him all these years? Honestly."

I shake my head. "Not really."

"I never wanted you to feel cheated out of having a dad. I only wanted what was best for you, and I really and truly thought that we would be just fine without Bill Davies in our lives. Things have been fine, haven't they? Most of the time?"

Mom is looking at me with such hope. She wants me to say that yes, we're fine. There is no way to know if our lives would have been better, but the truth is, they haven't been bad. At least no worse than anybody else's lives.

"We are fine."

This time Mom's smile is genuine. She tucks my hair behind my ear, like she has done a million times before, and asks gently, "Do you want him to be part of your life? He wants to talk about it."

"No."

Mom looks relieved, but because she is a good mom, she asks again. "Are you sure?"

"Well, maybe."

"We can work something out. He can come visit you; you could go visit him. It's up to you, baby."

"Do I have to decide now?"

"Of course not."

"I'd like to think about it."

Mom nods. "I think that's a good idea."

I give her one more squeeze, then make my way to bed. I make it to the doorway before Mom pipes up one more time.

"Clarissa?"

"Yes?"

"Have you been drinking?"

I think about lying, but what's the point? We've both been so honest tonight. Why spoil it? "Sort of . . ."

"What does that mean?"

"It means I just had one cooler, and I called Denise to drive me home."

Mom thinks about this. "I'm not exactly happy about this, but you were right to call Denise."

"Am I in trouble?"

"Just this once, I'll let you off the hook. But if I were you, I'd drink a big glass of water before I went to bed. You'll pay for it tomorrow if you don't."

"Are you going easy on me because you feel bad about Bill?" I ask.

"Maybe a little. Now go to bed before I change my mind." After a moment she adds, "Please."

The please is new. I like it; it makes me feel like we're equals. Maybe after all this is over, Mom and I will emerge more like friends, with the kind of relationship that moms and daughters have on TV. That would be nice, though I still like having a mom. In a weird way, it's nice to know that someone cares enough about you to really let you have it. That being said, I'm glad she went easy on me tonight. There's only so much drama a girl can handle, and there's going to be a wedding tomorrow.

Wedding Day

"Rise and shine!"

When I manage to unglue my eyelids, I see Denise at my door, wearing my mother's ruffled apron and holding a spatula. The smell of a big breakfast wafts in from the kitchen, rousing me out of sleepiness. I yawn, stretch, then shuffle to the kitchen. I feel better than I have in ages. More settled. Less anxious. Plus, there are pancakes, bacon and eggs. How can you be anything but happy with pancakes for breakfast? Around here, it's a real treat. You're lucky if you can get anything more decadent than strawberry yogurt for breakfast.

I take three pancakes and three slices of bacon and cover the whole thing in maple syrup, making Mom groan.

"How can you eat that? I think I'm going to be sick," she scolds.

Denise ignores her, helping herself to the syrup. "It's important to eat a big breakfast the day of a wedding. I can't tell you how many brides run around all day not eating, and then feel faint by the time the dancing starts."

"First of all, this is a quiet, simple, backyard affair, and second of all, there probably won't be any dancing."

Denise looks hurt. "No dancing at a wedding? Impossible!"

"It's not that kind of wedding."

"We'll see, won't we, Clarissa?" Denise looks slyly at me over a forkful of eggs. "Maybe you'll want to dance with your man?"

Now Mom is looking at me, too. "Michael?"

I nod, strategically stuffing my face with pancakes so I don't have to answer.

After we eat, we go to the Hair Emporium to beautify. Denise pulls out her arsenal of makeup products, and Mom picks out three hairstyles for me to choose from. All three are complicated up-dos that are far more elegant than anything I've ever had done to my hair. On the counter, Mom has laid out a silver chain with a single pearl strung on it and a matching pair of pearl earrings.

"Any one of those styles will look great with the jewellery," she says. "And your dress, of course."

Despite the heat, the pearls feel cool and solid under my fingers, as if they've kept a little bit of that deep-sea chill of the ocean inside them. They're beautiful but not fussy. Maybe I'll start wearing earrings more often.

Mom does Denise's hair first, wrapping it in hot rollers, and then sitting her under the dryer so the curls can set. That's how dedicated Denise is to beauty: she's willing to sit under a hot dryer for twenty minutes in the sticky, soggy heat of August. She flips through a magazine while she waits, occasionally sharing the interesting bits with us. She has to yell over the drone of the dryer.

Mom pats the seat of the styling chair. "Your turn, baby."

I hold my own magazine in my lap, featuring my sophisticated-yet-simple hairdo of choice. Mom peers over my shoulder, memorizing the style.

"Perfect. Now head down, eyes closed."

I do as she says, and she works her fingers into my hair, kneading my scalp and the muscles at the back of my neck, until everything feels loose and tingly. Her fingers never get tangled in my hair, and her nails never once dig too sharply into my skin. Ten minutes or a whole day passes, I have no idea. Time gets wonky when you're in Annie Delaney's magic hands.

"All done. Head up, please."

I open my eyes to see Mom smiling at me in the mirror. I smile back.

"Hello, beautiful," she says. I could say the same to her. She is, and will probably always be, the most beautiful person I know. But now when I look at her, I don't just see the Dairy Queen or a stylist, or even my mom. I see a person with a past and secrets and feelings and thoughts that I will never know. She's not perfect or untouchable; she's just a person, like me. But she is the most important person in the whole world. I smile back at her.

"Hi, Mom."

***

Eighteen people turn up ready for a barbeque, bringing homemade salads, extra beer, chips and dip, even a whole watermelon. My job is to make sure that all the food makes its way to the card tables Doug set up side by side and draped in a tablecloth we never use. People laugh and talk, happy to be out in the sun socializing on a Sunday afternoon.

Everyone wants to know where Mom is.

"She'll be out soon," I promise.

When Mattie arrives, she takes one look at my dress and her eyes grow three sizes. "Oh my gosh," she says. "Look at you! Are those pearls real?"

I'm so relieved to see her that I break with our tradition — this time, I'm the one that hugs her.

"I missed you," I say. She's wearing a cute sundress that is surprisingly lacking in bows, ruffles or lace. It's yellow, which makes her tan look even more impressive.

"What happened with you-know-who?" Mattie whispers. "I'm dying to know!"

"It's a long story," I say.

"A good one?" she asks hopefully.

"I'll tell you later. You look really sophisticated," I say. Then I catch sight of the seven or eight friendship bracelets she has on her right arm. "Well, except for those."

"One of these is for you." Mattie unknots a bracelet made with black and hot pink thread and ties it around my wrist. It feels soft and a bit warm from her skin.

"Thanks!"

Mattie beams and hugs me again. "You're welcome!"

I wonder how things would have turned out if Mattie had been here this week. Maybe she would have stopped me from heading to the Lilac Motel, or maybe she would have come with me and given Bill a piece of her mind. Whatever the outcome, I know she always has my back. Anyway, there isn't much point thinking about it. You can't change the past.

"Where's Benji? What has he been up to all summer? He said he was going to write, but I never got a single letter!"

Benji hasn't arrived yet. It's the one soft spot in a perfect apple of a day. I don't understand where he could be. There is no way he forgot, and even if he did, he lives right next door. Surely he can hear all the people milling about in our backyard.

"He's not here yet."

175

"And Michael?"

"He's filling a plate."

We both turn to look at the food table, where Michael is struggling to balance his already full plate with one hand and scoop potato salad with the other. The tips of his ears are bright red. I guess he didn't listen to his mother's lecture on sunburned ears.

"Are you guys official?"

"I think so."

"That's not very convincing. If you were official, you wouldn't have to think about it."

I'm not in the mood to dissect Michael's behaviour, so I excuse myself to go check in with Doug. I have to stand around and pretend to laugh with his gym buddies until he can step away for a second. We haven't spoken about the time he gave me heck for letting his dog pee on the floor. But after yesterday's heart-to-heart, if he's okay with letting it go, then so am I.

"How do I look?" Doug asks. He's wearing khaki pants and a white shirt and smells like aftershave — but the nice kind, not the horrible cheap stuff that teenagers wear. I had no idea he owned such nice things. I only ever see him in gym clothes and jeans.

"Handsome," I say.

Doug smiles. "And you look gorgeous."

"Are you ready?" I ask.

Doug pats his breast pocket, where he's stashed the ring.

"Ready as I'll ever be."

"I'll go get her."

By 3:15 everyone but Benji has arrived. I can't believe that whatever is happening between Benji and me is so bad that he would miss my mother's wedding, but I can't stall any longer. When I get a chance, I slip inside and go get Mom and Denise, who are waiting patiently in the Hair Emporium.

Even though I spent hours with them getting ready this morning, the sight of them dressed up still catches me off guard.

"Everyone's here," I say.

Denise squeals a little and fusses over the chain of Mom's necklace. "This is it."

They both giggle, and I feel like I'm looking back through time, catching a glimpse of them as giddy teenagers. Denise attempts to fluff out Mom's skirt, even though there is no bustle and it's pretty tapered, so there isn't much to fluff.

Denise does a little bow. "After you, Annie."

After they both check their lip gloss one final time, we walk up the stairs, single file, me in the lead. I tell them to wait in the kitchen, out of sight, while I go let the officiant know we're ready. It's actually my mom's client Jen, who is licensed to marry people. I find her loitering on the porch, close to the screen door, waiting for my signal.

I wait for her to turn and see me, then I give her two thumbs up.

She returns the signal, gives me a wink and then taps a fork against her wineglass.

"Excuse me, excuse me. If I could grab your attention for a minute."

Gradually people stop talking and turn to look at her.

"Annie and Doug have asked me here today to join them in marriage."

Everyone cheers, and Doug's friends turn to him in shock, one of them roughing his hair up. Cripes. Didn't he hear the part about the wedding? Maybe now is not the best time to muss up your friend's — *the groom's* — hair.

"If I could ask you all to move to the side and clear a path, our bride and groom will join us."

Everyone is happy to oblige, and Jen walks down the porch stairs and across the backyard to the maple tree, the one I planted as a scrawny seedling when I was five. Not so long ago, it was barely a twig, thinner than a pencil with one tiny shoot. It's still not very big, but it's definitely a tree now, with branches and leaves and everything. It seems right that the wedding will take place under that tree, which is just as much a part of the Delaney women's history as anything else.

Once Jen takes her place by the tree, Doug follows, to many cheers and whistles. He turns and looks at the screen door expectantly.

"And now, the bride," says Jen.

Mom and I argued about music ever since she set the date. I know she wanted to be relaxed and non-traditional, but if you're going to walk down an aisle, even an imaginary one in your backyard, shouldn't there be music? I even made her a playlist of all the songs she could use, nothing too sappy or formal, just pretty songs by bands that she and Doug liked. And every time she said no.

So you can imagine how surprised I am when Benji steps out from the crowd, walks to the maple tree and starts to sing.

The song is "In My Life," by the Beatles, which was totally on my list. I'm not what you call an oldies fan, but I know both Doug and my mom like the Beatles. Plus the song is about remembering the past but looking forward to the future — perfect for a wedding, if I do say so myself.

Just before she leaves the kitchen, Mom turns to me,

winks and mouths, "Surprise!" Then she heads out into the backyard.

Denise and I follow a few steps behind, Denise smiling away and waving, like she's on the back of a float, and me staring at Benji, trying to swallow the great lump in my throat. As he sings, any lingering hurt or anger is washed away by a great wave of love. Maybe we don't spend every minute together anymore, and maybe we will disagree on things like coolers, but those mean nothing in the long run. I wish I could apologize right now, but instead I just smile at him and hope he can read my mind.

Once we get to the tree, Mom turns to hug us, as does Doug, then Denise and I both stand off to the side. "In My Life" ends, and Benji disappears into the crowd, Mom blowing him a kiss and Doug giving him a salute.

The ceremony is quick, maybe ten minutes. When Jen asks Doug to repeat after her, and then launches into "I, Douglas, take you, Annette," I get a weird urge to laugh. Watching my mom and Doug go through the steps of getting married, a ritual I've seen a hundred times on TV or in the movies, feels unreal.

When it's over, Jen turns the music back on, and everyone springs to life. Maybe it's my imagination, but the guests all seem brighter, more energetic, as if the wedding recharged them. The couples are standing closer together, stealing wistful glances at each other, and even the people who aren't paired off are more relaxed, laughing, helping themselves to more food.

I feel lighter than I have all week, as if the wedding flipped a big switch and light flooded my whole body, blasting away all the weird shadows, cobwebs and creepy things of the past few days. It's so easy to dwell on the bad stuff that sometimes you forget how good it feels to let it all go and move on.

It is in this supremely calm and wise state that I approach Michael, who is balancing two paper plates of food near the picnic tables.

"One of these is for you," he says. "The one with the plain hotdog."

"You remembered I don't like condiments."

"Except mayo. But there wasn't any, so it's plain. Sorry."

"It's perfect."

Any uncertainty about whether or not Michael and I should be official is gone. He knows how I like my hotdogs! That has to mean something.

"Michael, we're about to start high school."

"I know, in a week. Crazy!"

"And there is something I want to be sure about, you know, before we start."

"Okay."

"Are we . . . together?"

Michael's face turns pink, matching the tops of his ears, and my perfect mood wavers a little. Part of me wants to take it back, laugh and shout, "Just kidding," before things get even more awkward. Then we could go back to the way we were, which was fine. But a bigger part of me — the part that has learned that even if it hurts, the truth is better — forges on. "I know you said you weren't looking to date anyone for a while, and after The Dairy Bar Incident, I won't blame you if you say no. But I like you, and I thought you should know."

My cheeks may be burning, and I'm pretty sure my voice is higher than normal, but I feel great. Like an adult.

"Um, yeah, okay. I mean, if you want to."

That sounds positive, but I need to be absolutely sure. "Yes?"

Michael smiles his crooked smile that I love so much. "Yes. I mean, I sort of figured we were dating already . . ."

"Hey there, party people, am I interrupting?"

Charity flounces up beside us, wearing something black, pink and polka-dotted that looks more like a costume than a dress.

"What is that?" I ask, trying to sound more curious and less disgusted.

She does a twirl and poses. "You like? It's an old prom dress I found in the costume department at the theatre. So vintage, right?"

I laugh. "Only you could pull that off."

Charity leans forward and kisses the air beside my cheeks, one at a time. "Thank you, daaaahling. It's sweet of you to say."

"Michael, this is Charity. You might remember her from the play Benji was in. She was Dorothy."

"Wasn't your hair brown then?" Michael asks.

"It was a wig," Charity explains.

"You look like the girl from the Tim Hortons commercials, the—"

Charity cuts in, "The 'Roll up the Rim' ones? Yes, I am that same girl." She looks a little sheepish, but she covers it up by doing an exaggerated curtsy. I used to think she was stuck-up and full of herself, but it turns out Charity finds those commercials just as lame as everyone else does. For her, commercials are just a means to an end, cheesy but necessary pit-stops on the way to her goal of being a serious actress.

"And who might you be? Are you the famous baseball player Clarissa was telling me about?"

Now Michael is the one blushing, but in a pleased way.

"Yes, this is Michael," I hesitate, then add, "my boy-friend."

Michael sticks his hand out, and Charity shakes it, look-ing amused. "Why so formal? This is a wedding; give me a hug!" she cries, and pulls him into her arms. Over his shoulder, Charity winks.

As Michael and Charity chat, I scan the crowd for Benji. I want to apologize and tell him how wonderful his singing was.

"Dean! Over here!"

Charity has jumped up and is waving at the driveway, where Dean is peering over the fence, wearing enormous sunglasses, looking a little lost.

"I invited him to come. I didn't know it would be a pri-vate wedding. Is that okay?"

"Sure," I say. "So, you and Dean?"

Charity smiles, as satisfied as a cat. "Yeah. At least until he has to go back to school. Long distance never really works."

As Dean makes his way over, I spot someone darting through the kitchen door and into the house, quick and sneaky, like he doesn't want to be seen.

"I'll be right back," I say.

Then I follow Benji into the house.

Day of Truth

I find him downstairs in the Hair Emporium, lights off, fan on low, sitting in a stylist's chair with his knees pulled up and his face wedged between them.

"Benji?"

When he looks up, his face is blotchy red and wet with tears. "Please leave me alone." His voice is hot and tight, like a slap. I'm not used to hearing anything other than sweetness in his voice. Part of me wants to turn on my heel and do just as he says: leave him alone. But that's not what friends do. It's definitely not what Benji would do, so I force myself to stay.

"I don't want to. You're upset, and besides, this is my house, you can't kick me out."

Even that little bit of humour doesn't work. Benji buries his head back between his knees and moans, "Please, please just leave me alone."

I creep toward him and sit on the chair next to him, not making any sudden movements, as if Benji is a cat about to dart. "You were really good today, Benji. So, so good." I raise my hand, as if to pat his shoulder, but part of me knows he doesn't want to be touched, so I hover there for a bit before I'm able to say, "I think I know what this is about."

Benji's head snaps up so quickly that I'm taken aback. "You do?"

I say the next bit as gently as I can, knowing firsthand how much words can sting, "Charity and Dean."

Benji doesn't say anything, just keeps himself as still as possible, as if he is physically holding himself together. So I continue, "You know I like Charity and everything, but if you ask me, she'd be a high-maintenance girlfriend. Maybe she's better as just a friend."

Benji is still mute. I'm not good at consoling people. I feel all the right things, but I just can't translate them into the words that make things better.

"Besides, I thought you liked Dean."

"I do."

"And you like Charity."

"She's one of my best friends," Benji sniffs. "After you, of course."

"So isn't two of your favourite people dating a good thing?"

"I like Dean."

"And you like Charity, so this is kind of perfect."

Benji's hands curl into fists and he presses them into the sides of his knees. It's something he does when he's frustrated or frightened. "I don't like Dean the way I like Charity. I like Dean the way you like Michael."

He says it so quietly, I wonder if I made it up. I'm about to say something when the meaning of his words sink in, and I am left with no words of my own to talk back. Outside people are laughing and chatting, and music drifts through the open windows. Suddenly, that world seems far away. I sit absolutely still in my salon chair, afraid to say anything, in case it's the wrong thing to say.

I've never known a gay person before, or maybe I have and I didn't realize it. I think about how Benji has never really had friends who weren't girls, and how he loves chatting with Mattie about clothes. I think about how, for as long as I've known him, Benji has never admitted to having a crush. I think about how, in grade seven, Terry turned his life into a nightmare, and how much worse it must have felt for Benji knowing that, secretly, Terry was right about him.

"Does Dean know?"

"I don't think so," Benji says, then pulls his head into the neck of his shirt like a turtle. "I hope not. I'd be so embarrassed."

"He should be flattered!" I say, trying to inject a little lightness into the conversation, which is getting heavier by the second. "You're a catch!"

Benji doesn't even smile. I want to touch him, bump his shoulder or give his hand a squeeze, but he's practically withdrawn into his clothing, and I'm afraid that if I do touch him, he'll jump right out of his skin.

"Dean is cute. Maybe a little too old for you, but I can see how you could have a crush on him."

Benji sniffles, but doesn't look up. I want him to look at me so he can see that things are okay. I've known Benji since we were seven years old. I am probably the person who knows the most about him. He's definitely the person who knows the most about me: the good stuff and the bad. Knowing one more thing about him doesn't change all the other stuff I know to be true. He's still the same Benji, the one who doodles comic masterpieces all over his math book, prefers blue-raspberry slushies (like me), struggles with a stubborn cowlick at the top of his head and giggles into his hands when he's excited. It doesn't feel like anything has changed, more like something has clicked, like a piece I didn't even know was missing has now been found.

No matter what happens, we are still Benji and Clarissa. No crush, boy or girl, can change that.

"I'm glad you told me."

More sniffling.

"Benji, will you please say something? Anything?"

He wipes his face with the hem of his shirt, like a little kid. "Please don't tell anyone."

"Of course not," I assure him. "I would never tell your secrets to anyone."

Finally, he smiles. It's a little baby smile, but it's there. "I know."

"Do you want to go back up?"

Benji takes a shaky breath. "Do you?"

"Not yet."

"Me neither."

"Scooch." Benji shuffles over, and I squeeze myself in the space he's created and take his hand. After a moment I squeeze it, then he squeezes back. We do this back and forth a few times, each of us trying to squeeze before the other does, until Benji starts to giggle.

"Not so hard," he says.

I'm not really a hugger, but I have an urge to squeeze him so hard for all those times he couldn't share his secret, and for all the times to come that will be difficult. I want him to know that I love him and will be the Denise to his Annie, only with less makeup and better jokes. Sometimes you can say things with a hug that you can't say with words. I squeeze Benji's hand one final time until he yelps.

He pulls his hand away and shakes out the pain. "Break my hand, why don't you," he complains, but he's smiling as he says it.

"I only squeeze as hard as I love," I say, half-joking.

Benji grins. "That sounds like something Doug would say. Are they doing speeches?"

"They weren't going to."

"I bet they will. People demand speeches at weddings."

"And when did you become such a wedding expert?"

"I *am* a wedding singer now."

I roll my eyes. "Of course. That must be it."

Benji and I grin at each other.

"Upstairs?" I ask.

Benji nods. "Upstairs."

We struggle out of the chair, which is not supposed to accommodate two people, straighten our non-wedding finest and head back up to face everyone. Benji grasps my hand until we get to the kitchen door, then he lets go and heads back into the world. My hand is clammy and throbs a little bit from the squeezing war. Maybe Benji's does, too. I hope that it does, and that when he sees Charity draped all over Dean, or Doug making googly eyes at my mother, or even me trying not to stare at my new, official boyfriend, Michael, he feels a similar throb in his own hand and is reminded that he is loved, too.

A Good Day

Benji was right. People have gathered on the porch and are insisting that Mom and Doug make speeches. Benji catches my eye, raising his eyebrows slightly to give me his I-told-you-so look. I shrug, like I knew all the time this was happening.

Michael comes to stand beside me, and all the little hairs on the arm next to him zing to attention, while the butterflies in my stomach start swirling. I guess even when you're official, you can still feel nervous.

Mom starts, "Thank you all for coming. I didn't want to make a big fuss, but seeing you all here, I'm glad that Denise convinced me to have a little bit of a fuss." People laugh and raise their glasses to Denise, who beams so big, my cheeks hurt just looking at her smile.

"I've been lucky in a lot of ways. I have a beautiful, smart daughter who challenges me to be a better person every day, and a friend who is as loyal as they come. I have this wonderful salon and all of you beautiful people who let me style your hair. I have my health—" Mom's voice catches on that last word. She presses her hand to her chest, swallowing any tears she may have.

A tear springs to my eye, instead, and I wipe it away quickly. I'm thinking of the time she had breast cancer and how every day I thought she might die. She's healthy now, but sometimes, when I watch her car pull away, or she calls to schedule a check-up with the doctor, I remember that at any time people can drop out of your life — and not just people who have been sick. Like Benji's mom.

Mom has recovered and continues. "That's more than many people have. Not so long ago, I would have said that I had enough. I certainly didn't feel like I was missing out on anything. But then I met you, Doug, and now I can't imagine life without you. You are kind, gentle and forgiving, and I will go forward from this day doing what I can to deserve you."

Doug has to clear his throat and wipe a man-tear from his eyes before he can speak. When he does, he takes Mom's hands in his giant paws. All around them, other people are sniffling, too.

"Annie. I'm so much better with you. I can't believe you agreed to share your life with me, and I swear I will be your partner in every possible way. I promise to love you and support you and your amazing daughter, Clarissa. You're my family now, and my top priority. I promise to treat you with respect, let you take the first shower every morning, pick the radio station in the car and decide what movie to go to on date night. Clarissa, I want to thank you for trying so hard to keep me cool. You're always telling me what's lame and what's not, and I appreciate it. I'm sorry to say this next bit may sound a bit lame to you, but sometimes even the lamest jokes have a bit of truth in them. A wise man once said that yesterday is history, but today is a gift. That is why it's called the present."

A few people chuckle. I am one of them. Even when he's serious, Doug can't help but be a little goofy.

"Annie, you have given me the greatest gift by agreeing to marry me today. I promise you a lifetime of living in the present."

Mom is smiling, even though her eyes are wet with tears, and when they hug each other everyone cheers. Despite the light feeling in my bones, I find my eyes are a little damp, too.

When I catch Denise she mimes wiping her eyes, rubs her fingers together in a gesture that means money, then points at me. So I lost the bet. It seems like a good one to lose. Besides, it's nice to let Denise win once in a while. It can't feel good to lose to someone half your age all the time.

* * *

The party goes late, and after the last guest is gone, we all come in — me, Mom and Doug, and Suzy, of course.

Suzy is locked in the kitchen for the night. As usual, she barks long after we've gone to bed. After a while, the barking becomes whining. She sounds so pitiful, I make my way to the kitchen, thinking enough is enough. Maybe if I give her a bone, or one of her disgusting, greasy little treats, she'll calm down, and we can all get some sleep.

The minute she sees me, Suzy's tail starts wagging a million miles an hour. She presses her face against the baby gate Doug set up to keep her in the kitchen, her little black nose poking through. Her sleeping pillow, which is giant and looks more like an inner tube than a dog bed, is lying unused in the middle of the kitchen. I step over the baby gate and sit on the floor next to her, cross-legged. Suzy launches herself into my lap and settles in, huffing into my pyjama pants. I'm not her favourite person, but I guess, in a crisis, even I will do.

"*Shhh*. You have to be quiet," I whisper, petting the soft warm space between her floppy ears. I like the feeling of the wiggly, solid warmth of her in my lap. It makes me feel responsible and protective. Suzy isn't picky — she'd be just as grateful to any stranger who offered her a bit of love. But right now she's happy because of me. It makes me feel a little bit gooey on the inside.

Eventually, Suzy's eyes droop, and she falls asleep, making funny little snoring noises. Very slowly, I pick her up and put her in the centre of her dog bed. She doesn't open her eyes or wake up even a little. I wait for a minute, just to make sure she's sound asleep and won't feel abandoned again when I tiptoe off to bed. When I'm absolutely sure, I whisper, "See? You're going to be just fine."

Tomorrow

Dear Bill,

Mom gave me your email address, but I decided to write to you because my friend Mattie says that things mean more when they are written down on paper. She spends every summer writing letters, so I figure she would know. I'm sorry I surprised you at the Lilac Motel. I honestly thought you would be happy to see me. I was so determined to meet you that I didn't think about what would happen after. I know now that my actions have changed your life forever, too. It must be weird to know you had a secret daughter all this time. At least I knew you existed.

I know that you must be mad at my mom because of the Jack thing, and because she kept me a secret from you. I was mad at her, too. But she is a very good mother, and I'm sure you did stupid things when you were younger, so I hope you can give her a break.

I thought maybe you would like to know a bit about me. My life has been good so far. Most of the time, it's been very good. I am an okay student. I've never broken any bones or had any major surgery. I used to think I wanted to be an actress, but now I think I might like to try something else, like directing. I like the idea of being in charge. Plus, when you are an actress, you have to take any part you get, even the lame ones. My friend Charity is an actress, and she has some pretty bad stories about some of the commercials she's done.

My best friend's name is Benji. He lives next door and is the nicest person I know. His mother died when he was four, and his dad isn't exactly the sensitive type, so things haven't always been great for him. He used to be really shy, but now he's into theatre. I know you don't know him, so you can't understand how crazy it is to watch him get up and sing in front of people. He even sang at Mom's wedding.

Oh yeah. Mom got married, to the guy you almost punched at the tournament. He owns his own gym and has a dog and is cool with me writing you, even though a lot of men would probably be threatened by it. Doug isn't threatened by anything. I'm trying to be more like that.

I also have a boyfriend, Michael. He plays baseball, like your nephew. That's why I was at the tournament that day, to cheer Michael on, not to spy on you, though I did think that maybe we would run into each other. I'm sorry that ended badly, but if that didn't happen, then I wouldn't be writing this letter, so maybe it was a good thing.

I've been thinking about your offer, and whether or not I want you to be part of my life. I used to wonder what it would be like to have a dad, but since I've never had one, I didn't feel like I was missing something. For now, maybe we could write each other sometimes. Real letters, not email. Maybe someday I'll come to Vancouver, and we can have dinner and get to know each other in person. I'd like that. You can write back or not write back and either would be okay. *I hope you won't be offended when I say I don't need you to feel happy or complete. Mostly I feel pretty lucky, but only on days that end in y.*

Sorry, lame joke, but sometimes even the lamest jokes turn out to be true.

Sincerely,

Clarissa Louise Delaney.

Acknowledgements

This day would not have come without the support and hard work of many people. There are scenes in this book that I have wanted to write since *Words That Start With B*, but my characters were not ready to experience them yet. I am grateful to the Scholastic Canada team who have been so generous as to allow me three books for Clarissa and Benji to grow.

Special thanks to everyone who not only helped realize the world of these books, but helped an author realize a dream: Mom, Dad, Jacqui, Cathy Francis, Nina McCreath, Denise Anderson, Stella Grasso, Maral Maclagan, Diane Kerner, Jennifer MacKinnon, Anne Shone, Nikole Kritikos, Cali Hoffman, Sally Harding and Kallie George.